'Haven't I seen you somewhere before?' Rob asked.

Seen me? You've danced with me, you've held me in your arms, Karen thought indignantly.

But, before she could say anything, Ross's brow cleared.

'But of course,' he said. 'I'm so sorry—Staff Nurse——?'

'Taylor,' Karen filled in for him, a little stiffly.

'Unforgivable of me,' the doctor said cheerfully, 'but people look so different in uniform.'

'I suppose they do,' Karen agreed. And she knew, then, that he hadn't realised that the girl he had danced with at the Hospital Ball was the staff nurse he saw every day in Women's Surgical.

Elisabeth Scott, who was born in Scotland and now lives in South Africa, is happily married, with four children all in their twenties.

She has always been interested in reading and writing about anything with a medical background. Her middle daughter is a nursing sister, in midwifery, and is her consultant not only on medical authenticity, but on how nurses feel and react. She wishes she met more doctors like the ones her mother writes about!

Previous Titles

GIVE BACK THE YEARS
HEBRIDEAN HOMECOMING

AND DARE TO DREAM

BY
ELISABETH SCOTT

MILLS & BOON LIMITED
ETON HOUSE   18–24 PARADISE ROAD
RICHMOND   SURREY   TW9 1SR

*First published in Great Britain 1991
by Mills & Boon Limited*

© Elisabeth Scott 1991

*Australian copyright 1991
Philippine copyright 1991
This edition 1991*

ISBN 0 263 77371 X

*Set in 10 on 12 pt Linotron Times
03-9108-51062
Typeset in Great Britain by Centracet, Cambridge
Made and printed in Great Britain*

CHAPTER ONE

AT LEAST it isn't raining, Karen told herself cheerfully, as she looked out at the grey Edinburgh morning.

She had to look out and up, because her flat was a basement one. Even then, pavement and feet were all she could see—but the pavement was dry today, and the feet weren't splashing through puddles. And, basement or not, it was near the hospital.

With the speed of long practice she put on her uniform, brushed her hair, grabbed her toast as it popped up, and made a large mug of tea.

She had forgotten to get out the marmalade, and as she turned to the cupboard she almost fell over William.

'Sorry, but you know very well you mustn't get in my way when I'm in a hurry,' she told him severely.

William wagged his tail apologetically. He was a big dog—too big, Karen knew, for a small basement flat—too big really for a girl who was only five foot three to manage. But she hadn't known he was going to grow so big, and, by the time she did, she couldn't have parted with him.

She looked at the clock as she stacked her dishes in the sink. Just time to give William five minutes across the road, in the park.

'Morning, Nursie,' the old man who sold newspapers called to her as she hung on to William's lead and tried to persuade him the five minutes was up.

'Morning,' Karen called back breathlessly. 'Come on, William, I'll be late. Home, boy!'

Once again she'd make it, but only just, she realised as she said goodbye to William, locked her door, and ran up the basement steps.

At the far side of the park—Inverlochy Gardens, to give it its proper name—stood the hospital, large and solid and sprawling. St Margaret's. And in spite of the grey autumn day, and the chill of the rain that would surely come later, Karen's heart lifted as she hurried through the park.

It was all so different from her home in sunny Cape Town, and the world-famous hospital where she had trained, but St Margaret's was where her grandmother had trained, and from the time Karen had decided to become a nurse she had known that she wanted to come to Edinburgh, to St Margaret's some time.

She had been here for just over a year now, and although there were times when she missed her family, and her home on the slopes of Table Mountain, and the sunshine, she loved Edinburgh, and she loved being part of St Margaret's.

'Come on, lass, Sister's ahead of you,' the porter told her as she hurried through the wide stone gateway.

Fortunately, Sister must have stopped off somewhere on the way, for there was just time for Karen to throw off her cloak, straighten her cap, and join the rest of the day staff on Women's Surgical before she heard the familiar brisk tap of Sister Newton's feet coming along the polished corridor.

'She almost caught you this time,' Karen's friend Moira whispered to her, as Night Sister began her report.

'You don't mind if we begin, Nurse Sullivan?' Sister Newton asked pleasantly. 'Thank you.'

The night had been fairly uneventful, and that was unusual in a surgical ward, Karen thought as she listened to the report. No drains had become dislodged, there had been no unexpected haemorrhages, the two gastric resection patients had had no further problems with blood-pressure or respiratory rates, and the appendectomy patient had reported a return of peristaltic sounds.

'The peritonitis is obviously subsiding, and we can reduce the parenteral fluids, but no food or fluid until the temperature and pulse-rate fall further,' Night Sister said.

She smiled, and Karen thought she looked tired, in spite of the quiet night.

'I'm afraid you have an admission coming very soon, Sister Newton,' she went on. 'Motorbike accident— the young man has a fractured femur; his passenger has head injuries. Mr Cameron is operating now, and she'll be brought to us as soon as he's finished.'

Mr Cameron.

In spite of all her determined resolutions, Karen's heart turned over. But which Mr Cameron?

'Ross or Adam?' Sister Newton asked, her voice low.

'Ross—he was on call,' Sister Black replied.

Which meant, Karen knew, that Ross Cameron would be in and out of the ward throughout the day, conscientious as he always was about his patients.

'Staff Nurse Taylor,' Sister Newton said, as Night Sister left, 'see that everything is ready for Mr Cameron's patient. I'll ring Theatre and find out how soon she'll be brought to us.'

Methodically, Karen checked the bed the new patient would be brought to. The wall unit of oxygen was full, the suction machine ready, and the drip stand. There was a baumanometer ready, and she collected from the duty-room the charts that would be needed, for there would have to be a complete record of neurological signs.

When she was satisfied that everything was ready, she went back to Sister Newton's office.

'Thanks, Staff,' Sister Newton said. 'I've just been talking to Mr Cameron—he wants her kept in the recovery-room until they can remove the endotracheal tube, and decide whether she needs mechanical ventilation or not.' She sighed. 'She wasn't wearing a crash helmet. They just went for a spin, the young fellow said. He's in better shape than she is, it seems.'

'Doesn't Mr Cameron want this girl kept in ICU for a while?' karen asked.

'Oh, yes, he would prefer that, and so would I,' the older woman returned. 'But they're short-staffed there in any case, and with this flu around it's even worse. We can't even special her, but at least we're better staffed than over on Men's Surgical.'

With no immediate hurry for the patient from Theatre, Karen joined Moira and the other nurse in the familiar ward routine. There were dressings to be changed, temperatures taken, blood-pressures recorded, the bedpan round, all before the patients were ready for breakfast.

'A new patient coming in, Nurse?' asked old Mrs MacIntyre, as Karen checked her wound—she had had a gastric resection—and filled in the drainage evaluation on her chart.

'Yes, a young girl who's been in a motorbike accident,' Karen told her.

'And young Mr Cameron operated on her, I hear?' the old lady said.

'There isn't much you don't hear,' Karen replied, as she carefully positioned the old lady in the semi-recumbent position that would help her to digest her food without suffering from the dumping syndrome so often experienced by patients who had had gastro-intestinal surgery.

'Thanks, lass. Och, well, there isn't much to do but listen to what's going on,' Mrs MacIntyre said cheerfully.

Breakfast was over, and the ward settled down again, when one of the theatre nurses brought the new patient.

'Epidural haematoma,' the nurse from the recovery-room explained as she and Karen carefully moved the unconscious girl from the trolley to the bed. 'And Mr Cameron wants her in Sim's position.'

The two nurses got the young girl on her side, with her head supported on a pillow. Her injury was on the right side of her head, and her long fair hair had been shaved off. That would distress her when she realised it, Karen knew. And she knew, too, that that would be a good sign.

'Mr Cameron said he'd be up soon, to talk to Sister,' the nurse from the recovery-room said. 'I have to get back now.'

She had only just gone when Karen, putting another pillow under her patient's flexed knee, heard swift sure footsteps coming towards her. Ross Cameron—she knew, without turning round, that it was him.

'Sister is on the phone; she'll join us,' he said

brusquely, and his dark eyes assessed his patient. 'I want Sim's position because I'm not too happy about her breathing,' he added. 'Nice, thanks, Staff. I'm prescribing indomethacin suppositories to reduce the risk of hyperpyrexia, and I want IV therapy maintained until she can take naso-gastric feeds. Tomorrow we'll increase the fluid and correct the electrolyte balance.'

His thick fair hair was untidy from wearing his theatre cap, and he ran his hand wearily through it.

'Silly young fools, both of them,' he said, anger in his voice. 'The boy had a crash helmet, but she didn't. I'll be back later, Staff. Oh—her folks live in Aberdeen, they've been sent for.'

He strode back down the ward, and Karen, watching, saw Sister come out from her office to talk to him. She turned back to her patient.

Jenny Robertson. Seventeen years old, the chart said.

And Karen, looking at the girl lying unconscious in the hospital bed, her head bandaged, was as angry as Ross Cameron had been at the unnecessary extent of the damage.

He was a good surgeon. She hadn't ever worked in Theatre, but she'd spoken to girls who had, and they all said Ross was just as good as his brother Adam. But Adam was older—thirty-eight to Ross's thirty-two, apparently—and Adam was the chief of the surgical team they were both part of. Karen had sometimes thought that perhaps it wasn't too easy for either Adam or Ross, being on the same team.

Somehow, as it often did, the day seemed to gain momentum after that. Tea and coffee came for the patients who were able and allowed to have it, and Sister told Karen to take a tea-break herself. There was no time to go down to the staff canteen, but Karen, hurrying along to the duty-room found that Moira had seen her coming, and made her a cup of instant coffee.

'And what was our Ross glowering at?' Moira asked, sitting on the windowsill, her long slim legs swinging.

'He was angry because this kid didn't have a crash helmet on,' Karen explained.

'Better than being angry with you, anyway,' Moira returned.

I don't know, Karen thought, surprising herself. At least he'd notice me! 'Thanks, Staff. Well done, Staff.' And that's the extent of it.

'I prefer Adam, of course,' Moira went on. 'He's better looking, and he's—more sure of himself, somehow. I wonder if he'll be at the Ball?'

The annual Hospital Ball was in a few days' time. Karen hadn't gone to it last year because she was so new that she'd hardly had time to get to know anyone. But this year it would be fun, going in a group of nurses and doctors she knew.

'Isn't everyone supposed to put in an appearance?' she asked Moira, as she finished her coffee and stood up. 'So Adam Cameron is bound to be there.'

Moira laughed.

'Sure, and isn't our Adam a law unto himself?' she asked, her Irish accent deliberately more pronounced. 'Ah, well, a girl can dream.'

'Come on, Moira,' Karen said affectionately. 'You know the minute Ian qualifies you'll get married.' She looked at her fob watch, pinned on to her uniform. 'We'd better get a move on; it's almost time for the doctors' rounds.'

Today it would be only Adam Cameron and his team coming, because the other surgeon, Mr Wilson, was operating. Karen had just finished checking that everything was in order when she heard Sister Newton greeting the surgeon.

'No, no problems, Mr Cameron,' she said, as Karen fell into line in an appropriately humble position towards the back. There were three medical students with the team, and as Adam Cameron shot some questions at them Karen gathered they had been in the theatre gallery watching this morning's emergency operation.

'Quite impressive, I gather, Ross,' he remarked to his brother.

Karen wondered if she had imagined the momentary tightening of the younger surgeon's lips.

'I had to work fast,' he replied. 'There was a very real danger of thrombus formation.'

Adam Cameron took the chart Sister Newton handed him, and studied it.

'I don't know that I'd have used Sim's position,' he said thoughtfully.

'It was the possibility of respiratory complications that made me feel better drainage was necessary,' his brother returned evenly.

Adam Cameron looked down at the girl on the bed for a few minutes, then he nodded, and moved on.

When the ward round was over, and the surgeon and his team had gone, Sister Newton sent Karen and Moira off for early lunch.

'And get out for some fresh air before you come back,' she told them. 'I can't afford to have anyone going off with this flu.'

'She's not a bad old stick,' Moira said, as they took the lift down to the staff canteen.

'She's not so old,' Karen protested. 'I heard she was forty-two.'

'That's old enough,' Moira returned blithely, with all the arrogance of her twenty-three years. 'Salad for me—nothing's going to stop me getting into that black dress for the Ball!'

They joined a group of girls at a big table near the window, and found that all the talk was of the Ball, who was partnering who, what everyone was wearing. Karen, half her thoughts on the girl lying unconscious in the ward, was only half listening, until she heard someone say 'Mr Cameron'.

'Whose girl is she, anyway?' Helen Jones wanted to know.

'She's Adam's girl,' Moira Sullivan replied, with certainty. 'Ian and I saw them going off in his car a couple of days ago; he had his arm around her—oh, yes, she's Adam's girl, although I hate to admit it.'

'Well, I've seen her with Ross too,' Helen insisted. 'And looking very friendly. They were walking along Princes Street—I couldn't swear he was holding her hand, but I think he was.'

Karen looked up from the mashed potato she had been tracing patterns on.

'Is this this artist you're talking about?' she asked carefully. 'I haven't seen her, but I've heard she's very pretty.'

'Yes, if you like the fair-haired, blue-eyed type,' said red-haired Moira, a little aggressively. And then, grudgingly, 'Well, I suppose she is pretty, but she looks very young, much younger than either Ross or Adam.' She stood up. 'Anyway, we'll see which Mr Cameron she comes to the Ball with. Coming for some fresh air, Karen?'

There wasn't much time, in the next few days, to think about the Hospital Ball, or to wonder which Mr Cameron this unknown girl would come with. Women's Surgical was busy, with three admissions operated on by Mr Wilson that morning, and all the beds were full. The accident girl, Jenny, drifted in and out of consciousness, and Karen felt so sorry for her mother and father as they sat anxiously by her bedside and waited for her to recognise them.

'I should never have let her come to stay with Wilma; it was her brother that took Jenny on the bike,' Jenny's mother sighed worriedly. 'If she'd stayed at home, this would never have happened.'

Karen couldn't help thinking that Jenny might just as easily have got on to someone's motorbike without wearing a crash helmet in Aberdeen, but she didn't say that. Instead she reminded the girl's mother that Mr Cameron had said Jenny was holding her own, and there were no signs of neurological damage.

Ross Cameron was in and out of the ward frequently. He was always pleasant and polite to Karen, thanking her as she anticipated what he needed, once even mentioning how meticulous her chart was. But he doesn't really see me, Karen thought. I'm part of the furniture, like the bed, or the drip stand, or the trolley.

Not that she really expected anything else, especially knowing about the girl with long fair hair, but what had Moira said? A girl can dream.

And just for a moment, as she looked at herself in the mirror before going to the Ball, she did dream.

She looked at her shining brown hair, curling now that it was released from her cap, and her dark brown eyes. Her dress was a deep rose, and it brought a matching rose to her cheeks.

'Staff Nurse Taylor—but I would never have known you!' she said to herself aloud.

'Oh, come, Mr Cameron, you see me every day,' she replied demurely.

In the mirror, she caught sight of William, wagging his tail because he thought she was talking to him.

'You are a mutt,' she told him lovingly.

Outside, a horn blared imperiously. Her lift had come. She patted William, and told him to be a good boy and look after the house. His tail drooped, his ears drooped, and he curled up reproachfully in his basket.

The Ball was held in the huge staff canteen, transformed, with balloons, streamers, huge paper flowers. This is fun, Karen thought happily, and put all thoughts of Ross Cameron out of her head as two of the young interns argued about who was going to dance with her first.

It was halfway through the evening that she saw Ross Cameron's fair head. He was smiling down at the girl in his arms, and it was a moment before the swirl of the crowd allowed Karen to see the long fair hair, shining and smooth, on the bare brown shoulders, and hanging down over the smooth white sheath dress.

She is lovely, Karen thought. And yes, she is very young.

And for a moment, in spite of all her good resolutions, she couldn't help wondering how it would be to have Ross Cameron smiling down at her like that.

'Dance, Karen?' Tony Johnson asked her, but she shook her head, and he grabbed another girl's hand and took her on to the crowded dance-floor.

Then, as Karen watched, she saw Adam Cameron walk across towards his brother and the fair-haired girl. She couldn't, of course, hear what he said, but she saw him smile as he reached them, and put one arm possessively around the girl. Claiming her, obviously. The next moment they were dancing, and Ross Cameron strode away from them, his face like thunder.

Away from them, and towards her.

Karen's heart thudded unevenly. It was nothing more than chance, but suddenly he was beside her. For a moment he looked back at the dance-floor, and then, abruptly, he turned to her.

'Would you like to dance?' he said.

Karen knew very well why he had asked her. But she didn't care.

'Thank you, I'd love to,' she replied, and, with her head held high, she went into Ross Cameron's arms.

CHAPTER TWO

I'M DANCING with Ross Cameron, Karen told herself, hardly able to believe it. His arms are around me, and he's holding me close to him. Very close.

He danced well, and, although he was so tall, she felt comfortable in his arms. Comfortable? Oh, no, she thought with certainty as the word came into her mind. Comfortable was not the way she would describe her feelings right now.

But of course, she reminded herself sensibly, her brown head close to his chest, the only reason he was dancing with her was because Adam had claimed the fair-haired girl, and Ross, furious, had turned to the girl he happened to be near.

Like Everest, I was there, Karen thought. But you don't look a gift horse in the mouth.

The confusion of that picture was so funny that it was difficult to keep back a bubble of laughter. But a glance at Ross Cameron's firmly set chin convinced her that he wouldn't be likely to appreciate the joke.

His arms tightened around her, and she saw that close to them on the dance-floor were his brother Adam, and the girl with the fair hair. She felt Ross's chin touch the top of her head, as he nodded to them.

And suddenly there was a tight knot of misery in Karen's throat, because it was so different from the way she had dreamed of it. Oh, she had laughed at herself—a nurse, cherishing a wild passion for a good-looking doctor, for heaven's sake—but looking at

17

herself in the mirror before she came here, looking
into her own brown eyes, wide and full of dreams,
somehow it hadn't seemed impossible that some of
these dreams might come true.

But not like this. This wasn't any dream, this was
reality, and a reality that hurt more than she would
have thought possible.

The music ended.

'Thank you,' Ross Cameron said, pleasantly, formally. His hand was under her elbow, ready to take
her back to her friends, but she murmured something—
she wasn't sure what—and, pulling her arm free,
walked across the room, her head held high.

'Well!' Moira exclaimed, impressed. 'How on earth
did you manage that?'

Karen shrugged.

'I was there, and he wanted to dance, that's all. Did
I hear someone say the buffet is open now?'

'What did he talk about?' Moira asked.

'We didn't talk,' Karen told her, with complete truth.
In fact, she thought, he's said more to me over a
patient's bed than he did now.

And the next day, when Ross Cameron came up to
the ward to see the young accident victim, he completed his examination, then turned to her.

'Can we check tomorrow's theatre list, Staff? In the
duty-room?'

And Karen, taken aback, found herself following
him to the duty-room. It wasn't her job to check the
theatre list; he knew very well Sister had already done
that.

In the small duty-room, Ross Cameron turned to
her.

'I know,' he said, before she could speak. 'But I

wanted to talk to you, and, unconscious though she is, I'm never prepared to take a chance on what a patient is capable of hearing. Now, Staff, I want your opinion on how she's doing. Not the information on the chart, I can read that—I want to know what you think.'

Karen hesitated, gathering her thoughts together.

'Her motor ability is improving,' she said at last, carefully. 'I'm certain she tried to squeeze my hand today. And she did move her toes—there doesn't seem to be any paralysis. She hasn't made any real response to her parents' being here, but I do think she knows.'

Ross Cameron, sitting on the desk, smiled.

'Good,' he said. 'That ties in with my own impression. You're the one who's spent most time with her, and I wanted your opinion. Thanks, Staff.'

He went off along towards the lift, and Karen turned back to the ward. It wouldn't, of course, have been correct or professional for him to say anything more personal.

And what, in any case, would he have said? she asked herself sensibly.

I did enjoy our dance at the Ball, Staff?

No, the ward wasn't the place for even a remark of that sort.

Jenny Robertson's mother had arrived when she reached the far end of the ward, and she was sitting beside her daughter, looking anxious.

'Oh, Nurse, it is all right just to come in?' she asked. 'Sister did say we could come any time. I'm on my own now; her dad's had to go back—he's on the oil rigs, you know.' And then, her careful control slipping, 'Oh, Nurse, I was hoping Jenny would be a wee bit better today.'

'It takes time, Mrs Robertson,' Karen told her, as

she had so many times. 'Mr Cameron thinks there's an improvement.'

Was it her imagination, or was there the slightest flicker of the girl's eyelids?

'It's so awful to see her lying there like that, and her always so bright,' Mrs Robertson said unsteadily. 'And I keep wondering if she'll——'

How much more she was going to say, Karen didn't wait to find out. She took Mrs Robertson by the arm and took her next door to the sluice-room.

'Sorry, Mrs Robertson, but you mustn't talk like that,' she said firmly. 'If you want Jenny to get better—and I know you do—you mustn't worry her about her condition. Right now, all she needs is to know you're there, and to know that, although you're worried, you haven't given up on her!'

She hesitated. Should she say if, or when? She made up her mind.

'When she begins to get better, when she's able to ask how she's doing, that's different. Mr Cameron and Sister and I will answer any questions she has honestly.'

She knew that Ross Cameron believed in being truthful with his patients, and Sister Newton kept drumming it into her staff that they were always to listen, really listen, to their patients, to listen for the questions that perhaps weren't actually being asked, to be ready with a straight and truthful answer.

Karen herself, from her earliest nursing days, had felt that instead of preparing a patient for an injection, and saying brightly, This won't hurt, it was much better to say that it probably would hurt, just for a moment, but it was necessary.

'I'll try, Nurse,' Jenny's mother said doubtfully.

Karen smiled.

'You don't have to pretend you're not worried, Mrs Robertson,' she reminded the woman. 'It would be foolish to do that. All I want is for you to be more positive.'

'But does Jenny even know I'm here?' Mrs Robertson asked.

'I think she does,' Karen said firmly. 'I think she knows you're here, and I think it helps her, knowing that. Talk to her, hold her hand—has she any brothers or sisters?'

'Two wee brothers,' the girl's mother told her. 'And she's awful fond of them. They're staying with their granny just now.'

'Tell her that,' Karen suggested. 'She might be wondering.'

A little later, when she was changing a dressing for the woman in the bed next to Jenny's, she heard Mrs Robertson telling the still figure in the bed about wee Sandy wanting his grandmother's cat to be allowed to sleep with him.

She was still smiling about this when she went back to the duty-room, and Sister Newton, looking up from the desk, asked her to share the joke.

'Not really a joke, Sister,' Karen said, 'just something that pleased me.'

She told Sister what she had said to Jenny's mother, and how Mrs Robertson had dealt with this.

'I like that,' Sister Newton said. 'And like you, I'm certain it will help Jenny. Oh, that reminds me, Staff— tomorrow we have a patient coming up from Theatre; she's having elective surgery done on varicose veins. She's Down's Syndrome, and I want all of us to be particularly careful with her—make sure she understands what's going to happen, see that she knows where the bathroom is, let her know how long until visiting hour—I know I can rely on all of you. Oh— and Staff, I've found before with mentally handicapped patients, they like to help. If she wants to hand round tea, or tidy magazines, let her—she'll feel more at home then.'

I'm very lucky, Karen thought, to be working under Sister Newton. She thought of some of the sisters she had worked under, at home in Cape Town and here in Edinburgh, and she knew that there weren't too many with as enlightened and caring an attitude.

By the following day there was no doubt that young Jenny Robertson was improving. She responded to questions from her mother, and once, when Karen was checking her dressing, she opened her eyes. Her lips moved, and the blue eyes were anxious.

'Your friend?' Karen asked. 'He's going to be all right—he's in plaster, but I'll see if we can arrange for him to come and see you.'

The girl's hand fluttered, moving towards her hair, and Karen's heart lifted.

'Yes, your pretty hair had to be cut, Jenny,' she said. 'We're all sorry about that, but it had to be done. It's starting to grow already, though.'

When Ross Cameron came up later, she caught him outside the ward, and told him this. He listened, and, when she had finished, he smiled.

'I thought she was going to be all right,' he said then. 'It's always brain damage we're afraid of, with these epidural haematomas, and of course we're not out of the woods yet, but it does look hopeful. Thanks, Staff.'

He really does have a lovely smile, Karen thought, not for the first time. He doesn't give it too freely, but it's worth waiting for.

She had an afternoon off the next day, and it was a clear crisp autumn day, a perfect chance to give William a good run in the Gardens.

Karen pulled on her blue tracksuit, and her thick-soled shoes, with William whining with excitement beside her, knowing very well this was to be more than his usual quick walk. When she reached the door he was waiting, his ball in his mouth.

The wind caught Karen's soft brown curls, usually pinned up and restrained by her cap, as soon as they were out in the street, and already she could feel her cheeks glowing.

Beside her, William walked as sedately as it was possible for him to walk, on the lead, but every now and then a whiff of some exciting smell came to him and he dashed forward, almost pulling Karen off her feet.

'Taking him for a wee walk, Nursie?' old Sam with the newspapers asked, straight-faced. 'Or is he maybe taking you?'

'That's more like it, Sam,' Karen agreed breathlessly. In the open area in the middle, dogs were allowed to be off the lead, and thankfully she reached there, and released William. He bounded away, torn between wanting to make friends with a fat spaniel, and remembering that now Karen would throw his ball for him.

The ball won, and William was back, standing in front of her, his eyes intent on her face. Karen threw the ball, and he ran to retrieve it. And pity anyone in his way, Karen thought, shutting her eyes as he just missed the fat spaniel and his elderly mistress.

Soon he was back, the ball was dropped at her feet, and he was waiting eagerly for it to be thrown again.

Karen walked briskly for a bit before she threw it, determined she would have her exercise as well as William his.

Half an hour later she thought they had both had enough.

'Once more, then home,' she told William, and threw the ball, and while William was running for it, she turned towards the gate. She was never sure, afterwards, if this was what confused William, that she wasn't in the same place, or if he just took a fancy to another tracksuited figure. He certainly couldn't have thought it was her, because the other figure was considerably taller, the tracksuit was navy instead of lighter blue, and the figure was masculine.

Too late, Karen saw what was going to happen.

William bounded towards the man, and, in an excess of friendliness, put his paws on the man's chest. Taken by surprise, man and dog fell. When Karen reached them, William had one large paw planted on each side of the jogger's face, as he peered down.

'I'm so sorry,' Karen called breathlessly. 'He just wanted to make friends.'

'With friends like that, who needs enemies?' the man in the tracksuit returned.

Karen felt as if she too had been knocked off her feet.

It was Ross Cameron. Unbelievably, he didn't sound angry. Amused, but not angry.

'Get back, dog, and let me stand up,' he said to William.

'His name is William,' Karen told him faintly.

'Get back, William,' Ross Cameron ordered and there was such unmistakable command in his voice that

William not only got back, but sat down, waiting for the next order, as Ross got to his feet.

'William? That's an unusual name for a dog,' Ross commented.

'When I got him, he looked awfully like my uncle William—you know the way Labrador puppies wrinkle their foreheads when things puzzle them?' Karen asked him.

Ross looked at William.

'You're not trying to tell me you thought he was a Labrador?' he said.

Karen nodded.

'His mother was.'

'His father certainly wasn't,' Ross returned. He bent to pat William, and William closed his eyes in delight. 'What was he, I wonder?'

'The vet thinks Great Dane,' Karen told him.

William had heard enough of these discussions about his parentage to find them boring. He picked up the ball again and put it hopefully at Ross Cameron's feet.

'Sorry, fellow, I have to go back on duty,' the doctor said. He looked at Karen then—for the first time, really, Karen couldn't help thinking—and frowned. 'Haven't I seen you somewhere before?' he asked.

Seen me? You've danced with me, you've held me in your arms, Karen thought indignantly.

But, before she could say anything, Ross's brow cleared.

'But of course,' he said. 'I'm so sorry—Staff Nurse——?'

'Taylor,' Karen filled in for him, a little stiffly.

'Unforgivable of me,' the doctor said cheerfully, 'but people look so different in uniform.'

'I suppose they do,' Karen agreed. And she knew,

then, that he hadn't realised that the girl he had danced with at the Hospital Ball was the staff nurse he saw every day in Women's Surgical.

'Home, William,' she said, and clipped the lead on the big black dog's collar. When she straightened, she looked up at Ross Cameron. 'I hope you didn't hurt yourself when William knocked you over, Mr Cameron.'

'I'm fine,' Ross replied. Unexpectedly, he smiled, and his dark brown eyes were laughing. 'I'll certainly look out for you and William in future, though. I've just moved into a flat on the north side, but I didn't realise Inverlochy Gardens held so much excitement for joggers!'

He waved as he jogged off, but Karen had both hands on William's lead.

And in spite of a severe reminder to herself about Ross Cameron's undoubted interest in the girl with fair hair—Shona Macdonald, the all-knowing Moira had discovered her name was—she couldn't help feeling pleased at the prospect of further meetings with Ross Cameron.

William, who knew very well that he had behaved badly, for his beloved mistress had made it very plain before that knocking people over was Undesirable Behaviour, was pleasantly surprised to find himself warmly hugged when they got home.

'Thanks to you,' Karen said, giving William an extra biscuit, 'he does at least know who I am!'

And sure enough, on the ward the next day, just as Ross Cameron was leaving, more than pleased with young Jenny Robertson's steady improvement, he turned back.

'Oh, Staff,' he said casually, and waited until Karen

was close enough for him to speak in a low voice. 'How's my friend William—knocked anyone else over recently?'

And, without waiting for an answer, he walked away, laughter in his dark brown eyes.

'I'll help you, Nurse; I could sweep for you,' Agnes, the Down's Syndrome patient, offered eagerly, as Karen turned back.

'Thank you, Agnes,' she said, thinking of what Sister Newton had said, and knowing too that it was important for the young woman to move as much as possible, now that her varicose veins had been operated on. 'The floors were swept this morning, but I could do with some help giving the other patients tea. Could you help me with that?'

'Sure, Nurse, I'm good at helping,' Agnes told her. 'First Jenny's mum?'

'First Jenny's mum,' Karen agreed.

Mrs Robertson was a star, she thought gratefully, now that she understood how she could best help her daughter. She talked to Jenny, told her about family and friends, and when the girl managed to whisper something she leaned closer until she could hear. It was only when Jenny was asleep that Karen would sometimes see slow silent tears running down her mother's cheeks.

'But she's going to be all right, I know that now,' Mrs Robertson said fiercely to Karen when she left that day. 'See you tomorrow, Nurse.'

Karen didn't want to say anything yet, but they were hoping that very soon now Jenny could have some solid food, and Sister Newton had suggested to Ross Cameron that they allowed her mother to feed her.

'It will be good for both of them,' Sister Newton had said, and after a moment Ross agreed.

There was a new nurse on their ward the next day, Karen saw when she went on duty, a black girl, standing beside Moira. As soon as they left the duty-room, Moira brought her over.

'You two can get to know each other properly over tea,' she said, 'but you can at least say hello, since you're from the same part of the world—Patience, Karen comes from Cape Town.'

The black girl smiled.

'And I come from the Transkei,' she said. 'Moira, that's like saying that your home in Belfast is close to Paris, or maybe Rome!'

'I only know the Wild Coast,' Karen said, smiling. 'We used to spend holidays there—I loved it. Where did you train, Patience?'

'In Durban,' Patience told her. 'And you at Groote Schuur?'

Karen nodded, but there was no time to say any more, for Sister Newton was frowning at them.

The ward was busy, and old Mrs MacIntyre had to have continuous gastric suction established, and it was only when the old lady was comfortable again that Karen realised that Ross Cameron hadn't been up to the ward to see young Jenny Robertson. Strange, she thought, because, no matter how long his theatre list was, he always managed to come up, even for a few minutes.

Afterwards, she realised that it was around then that she became conscious of an atmosphere of tension, of anxiety. At the far end of the ward, she saw Sister Newton speaking to Sister Baynes from Men's Surgical. Sister Newton seemed to be asking something, and the older woman shook her head as she replied. Then the two sisters turned and went out of the ward together.

A few moments later Moira came in from the duty-room, and walked right down the ward to Karen.

'Have you heard?' she said, her voice low. 'Isn't it awful?'

'Heard what?' Karen asked, and she knew by her friend's face that it was something pretty bad.

'Adam Cameron has been in a car crash,' Moira told her. 'He's badly hurt—they don't know if he'll live.'

CHAPTER THREE

'HE'S in Theatre now,' Moira went on. 'Been there for hours, I heard.'

'And his chances don't look too good?' Karen asked, shocked and shaken at the thought of Adam Cameron lying unconscious on an operating table, and the theatre team fighting to save his life. His own theatre team, in the theatre where so often he himself had used all his skill to save lives.

'Apparently a lorry came out of a side-road and right into him, and his right leg is pretty much shattered,' Moira told her. 'He'd lost a lot of blood before they got him here, and he was in shock—no, it doesn't look good.'

'Who's operating?' Karen asked.

Moira's dark blue eyes met hers.

'Ross is,' she said evenly. 'Mr Wilson is there too, for the look of it, because of the close relationship, but it seems he was the one who said that if anyone could save Adam Cameron's life it was Ross.'

Neither of them had seen Sister Newton coming, but there was no reprimand for talking in the ward. The older woman's grey eyes held nothing but concern.

'There's nothing any of us can do at the moment,' she said to them quietly. 'I'll let you know when there's any further news. Meanwhile, we have work to do, and patients who need us.'

She went back to her office, and Karen and Moira

began to chart the two-hourly temps, both more chastened by Sister Newton's understanding than they would have been if she had given them a telling-off.

'But you know,' Moira whispered, when they were at the far end of the ward, 'they say that she and Adam were very friendly, quite a few years ago, It didn't come to anything, but maybe that's why she's never married.'

If that was so—and Moira wasn't very often wrong, Karen had discovered—it was even harder on Sister Newton than on the rest of them. To Karen herself, Adam Cameron was a rather distant figure, who came into the ward on his rounds, who could be charming and pleasant to the young nurses if he felt like it, but who could be extremely demanding, and extremely scathing if things weren't done to meet his very exacting standards.

No, she didn't know the surgeon well enough to feel anything on a personal level, but it was enough to know him and respect him through his work, and to feel shock and concern for him.

But even if she didn't really know Ross much better—one dance, which he didn't remember, and one meeting in the Gardens with William—her heart ached for the younger surgeon, with no time to recover from the shock of this terrible accident to his brother before he was thrown into using all his skill to try to save his brother's life.

It's a dreadful responsibility, Karen thought soberly, and in many ways it wasn't fair of Mr Wilson to have pushed Ross into operating. From what she had heard from nurses who had worked in theatre, it was probably true that Ross was a better surgeon than Mr Wilson, but what a weight for him to carry, if anything should go wrong!

It was an hour later before Sister Newton came to the far end of the ward and beckoned to her. Moira was already in the office, and the two junior nurses.

'I've just had news about Mr Cameron,' Sister Newton said, and Karen, remembering what Moira had told her, could see that it was an effort for the older woman to speak steadily. 'They've just brought him out of Theatre. Unless anything unexpected happens, he—is going to pull through.'

'Thanks be to all the saints for that!' Moira murmured piously. But Karen could see that there was something more.

'But they had to amputate his right leg below the knee,' Sister Newton went on. 'There was no possibility of saving it—in fact, I've just spoken to Mr Wilson, and he says if it hadn't been for Ross Cameron's skill and determination a more drastic amputation would have been necessary.'

A few weeks ago, Karen had seen Adam Cameron on the staff tennis courts, playing singles against his brother. Lean and tanned, his backhand stroke devastating, his footwork sure—and laughing, as he leapt over the net when he had won by two points. At the Ball, dancing with the girl with fair hair, holding her close to him, smiling down into her eyes. In the ward, here, striding in when he was short of time, impatient, sometimes arrogant. But so sure of himself, so confident. So—whole.

She looked at Sister Newton, and in her distress there was no thought for the older woman's seniority and professional distance.

'He won't know yet?' she asked unsteadily.

Sister Newton shook her head.

'He hasn't regained consciousness yet,' she replied. 'He'll be in the recovery-room for a few hours, and then in the ICU for at least twenty-four hours.' She looked around the young nurses. 'And then,' she said steadily, 'he'll be in one of the side-wards between us and Men's Surgical.'

The small side-wards were used by either Men's Surgical or Women's Surgical, and were two-bedded wards. Patients who were in need of special attention were put there. And, of course, Adam Cameron would undoubtedly need special attention, special care.

The whole hospital, it seemed, felt the shock and the sadness of what had happened to one of their leading surgeons. In the staff canteen, in the duty-rooms of every ward, there was talk of nothing else.

Later that afternoon Ross Cameron appeared, to do a ward round. There were two patients from the previous day's theatre that he needed to check on, but Karen had thought he would have asked Mr Wilson to do this. She could see that he was exhausted, and under considerable strain, as he conscientiously checked the wound evisceration of old Mrs Brown, who had had a gastric resection done, and adjusted the traction for young Molly Harris, who had been operated on for a fractured femur.

Then he led the way to Jenny Robertson's bed. There was no doubt now, Karen thought, that the girl was well on the way to recovery.

'You know what, Jenny?' Ross Cameron said, and Karen's heart ached for him as she saw him manage a smile. 'I think we could check with Mr Wilson and see if we can arrange a wheelchair visitor for you—I believe your young man is just about able to be moved.'

'He's not my young man,' Jenny said, and there was a wave of colour in her cheeks, so pale most of the time. 'We're just friends, Doctor.'

'Well then, it will be nice for you to see a friend,' Ross returned.

'Don't let him come when my mum's here—she's still mad at him. I keep saying it was just as much my fault, but she'll not have that,' Jenny said.

'We'll try to keep him and your mum apart,' Ross promised. 'See you tomorrow, Jenny.'

Sister Newton hadn't come out of her office, so Karen went to the door of the ward with Ross.

'Mr Cameron,' she said hesitantly, as he handed her back the charts he had been studying, 'I'm so sorry about your brother.'

'Thank you, Staff,' Ross Cameron replied, and she could hear that he must have had to say this many times since he came out of the theatre that morning. Then he looked at her, and his smile, although still weary, was real. 'I'm sorry, I was miles away. William's mistress, of course. I—thanks for your concern.'

Abruptly, then, he strode off down the long polished corridor, his white coat flying behind him.

The news of Adam Cameron, throughout the rest of that day and the next, was cautious. He was holding his own, it seemed, but would still be kept in Intensive Care.

Just after lunchtime the next day, Karen was summoned to Sister Newton's office.

'Mr Cameron is coming out of intensive care tomorrow morning, Staff Nurse Taylor,' Sister Newton said. She took her reading glasses off and put them carefully down on the desk. 'You know he'll be in one of the side-wards on this floor? Yes, I mentioned that yesterday. I'm sure you know how short-staffed they are on Men's Surgical, while we're better placed.'

Puzzled, wondering what this could have to do with her, Karen waited.

Unexpectedly, Sister Newton smiled. 'Mr Cameron—Mr Ross Cameron—has asked if I could spare you, to special his brother,' she explained.

'Me?' Karen asked, taken aback. 'He asked for me?'

There was a glint of humour in Sister Newton's grey eyes. 'The small brown-haired staff nurse, the one who has the big dog,' she said.

Karen could feel her cheeks grow warm.

'Fortunately,' Sister Newton said gravely, 'I know about your dog, so I knew which of my nurses he meant.'

She put her glasses on again.

'Mr Cameron has been impressed, it seems, by your care of young Jenny Robertson, and by the understanding you've shown.' She sighed. 'And, believe me, you'll need plenty of understanding to special Adam Cameron. I think it's only fair to remind you that he's not the easiest of men in the best of circumstances.' Her grey eyes were bleak now. 'And these circumstances will be very difficult. For him, for you, for Ross Cameron.'

She seemed to realise, then, that she had been speaking less formally, less professionally, than she usually did.

'For both Mr Adam Cameron and Mr Ross Cameron, I mean,' she said quickly. 'As well as for you. Do you think you can do it?'

Karen lifted her chin.

'Yes, Sister, I can do it.'

And, silently, she couldn't help adding—at least, I hope I can!

In what was left of that afternoon she spent some time with the patients who had become her particular responsibility, especially Jenny Robertson.

'Thanks for all you've done for me, Nurse,' Jenny said shyly. And then, round-eyed, 'Nurse Sullivan says you're going to be looking after my Mr Cameron's brother, that was in this terrible accident.'

'Yes, I am, Jenny,' Karen replied. 'But I'll still be on the same floor, and I'll come and see you when I can.'

She turned to go, but the girl in the bed caught her hand.

'Nurse, do you think Mr Cameron will remember what he said—about getting someone to bring Bob in here to see me?'

'I'm sure he will,' Karen assured her.

Jenny looked away.

'Not that I care, really,' she said brightly. 'I mean, I hardly know him. But his sister, my friend Wilma— she says Bob feels awful bad about what's happened to me, so I thought I could tell him, like, that it was just as much my fault as his.'

Karen put her hand over Jenny's.

'As soon as I get the chance,' she promised, 'I'll talk to Mr Cameron about it.'

It was raining when she went off duty and hurried across the Gardens. As she unlocked her door she could hear William's tail thumping his greeting from the kitchen. And when she opened the door he launched himself at her, his paws on her shoulders, peering anxiously into her face.

'Get down, you dope!' Karen told him, laughing. 'I

know you've missed me, and I know you're glad to see me, but this is ridiculous!'

William nudged her across to the back door, where his lead hung. I suppose I might as well take him now; I'm wet already, Karen thought.

The only other people in the Gardens were hurrying homewards, heads down, umbrellas up. Karen kept William on the lead until she reached the open space in the centre, then she let him off, and stood under a tree while he ran around. Not a day for joggers, she found herself thinking, and then, quickly, she told herself that she certainly didn't expect to see Ross Cameron every time she came into the park with William, just because it had happened once.

'Home, William!' she called.

In the distance, William wagged his tail, to show that he had heard her, then ran in the opposite direction, to show that he wasn't ready to go home yet.

'William!' Karen called sternly, and this time he realised she meant it.

Karen had meant to spend the evening writing letters, for she liked to write once a week to her folks in Cape Town, and she was due to write to a couple of friends as well. But somehow she couldn't settle to anything. She kept thinking of the man who would be her patient tomorrow, the man whose life would now be so drastically changed, so completely different.

She had to report to Sister Baynes on Men's Surgical when she went on duty the next morning, and, knowing that Sister Baynes and Sister Newton were good friends, she hoped she would find she was as happy working with the older woman.

Sister Baynes was plump and grey-haired, and she had a reputation for strictness where her staff was concerned, but Karen was relieved to see that her blue eyes were kind and concerned when she handed over Adam Cameron's charts.

'I thought you could do with time to see what's expected of you, Staff Nurse Taylor,' she said, 'so I got these from Intensive Care. Mr Cameron will be brought up in half an hour. I'll take you to his room now, and we'll check things together.'

Although there were two beds in the small side-ward, there was no other patient.

'As long as it's possible, we'll let Mr Cameron be on his own,' Sister Baynes said. And then, her Scottish accent becoming stronger, 'The puir man will not be wanting anything to do with anyone else's troubles, and him with enough of his own. Now, Nurse, as you'll see, we have a fracture board, and a divided bed, with the division over the stump. Here's your cradle, to elevate the bedclothes. You will, of course, be watching the stump for haemorrhage; you'll have the bottom of the bed elevated, and a tourniquet ready. Mr Ross Cameron will give you further instructions—he said he would be up later.'

'Sister Baynes,' Karen said hesitantly, 'Does Mr Adam Cameron know that his leg has been amputated?'

The older woman's blue eyes were warm and compassionate.

'I believe he's been told,' she said quietly. 'But he doesn't seem to have taken it in.' She sighed. 'Not that it's unusual for a patient to deny this, to say it's not possible. Especially an accident victim like this. An amputation that's planned and discussed—well, the patient has time to get used to the idea, time to do the denying before it happens. But this way——'

Unexpectedly, she patted Karen's hand.

'I'm afraid you'll be having a difficult time, lassie. If I can give you a word of advice—and this is from someone who's been a nurse since you were just a bairn, and also someone who has known Adam Cameron since he was a wild young intern—he'll need sympathy, he'll need understanding, but, at the same time, don't stand any nonsense from him!'

More than a little taken aback, Karen looked at Sister Baynes. The older woman coloured, and immediately became completely professional again, her voice brisk as she told Karen of the arrangements made for another nurse to take over from her when it was necessary.

'Everything understood, Nurse Taylor?' she finished, her voice businesslike. 'Any questions?'

'No, Sister. Thank you, Sister,' Karen replied demurely, fascinated by the glimpse she had had of a very real woman beneath the starched sister's uniform.

Ten minutes later two of the nurses from Intensive Care wheeled Adam Cameron in on a trolley. He was unconscious, and one of the nurses told Karen that he had been given a strong analgesic by injection half an hour previously.

'Is he in much pain?' Karen asked, her voice low.

The other nurse nodded.

'We've been keeping him under strong sedation,' she said. 'Mr Ross said he'd be up to see you as soon as possible, to give you his instructions. But every time Mr Adam comes out of sedation, he suffers terribly from paraesthesia.'

Paraesthesia. Pain in the non-existent limb, the limb that had been removed. Karen had heard of this, and patients she had nursed before had talked of it, and she had always thought it must be one of the hardest things for a patient, to feel severe pain in a limb that was no longer there.

Quickly, expertly, the three nurses transferred the unconscious man to the bed, and Karen adjusted the cradle to elevate the bedclothes. Once Adam Cameron stirred, and groaned, but he didn't wake, and she was grateful for that. When the Intensive Care nurses had gone, she checked the bandage below his knee and completed the chart with his temperature and blood-pressure.

She had just finished this when Ross Cameron came in.

'Chart?' he asked brusquely, and she handed it to him.

'His blood-pressure has stabilised now,' he murmured. 'He gave us some bad moments last night. Two-hourly checks, please, Staff.' He looked around. 'Did they bring sandbags? No? I'll get Sister Baynes on to that.'

He strode out, and she heard him speaking to Sister Baynes. A few moments later he was back, carrying sandbags himself.

'You know how to use these, Staff?' he said to her. 'Roll them in a folded drawsheet from both ends, so that you keep the limb between the sandbags and beneath the drawsheet. From tomorrow, I want him flat on his back for short periods, to straighten his hips. As you see, I've splinted the leg, to prevent flexion contractures of the hip muscles.'

His instructions for analgesics were written out, and he went over this with her. When he had finished he stood for a while, not saying anything, looking down at his brother.

'He'll probably argue with you,' he said unexpectedly, 'about injections, about his treatment, about any damn thing.' All at once he looked exhausted, and Karen's heart went out to him. 'I'll be glad when he does,' he said, his voice low. 'In all my life I've never seen Adam like this.'

He turned away.

'I have to go back to Theatre now,' he said, professional and distanced again. 'I'll be up later. If there's any emergency, you won't be able to get me in Theatre, but get hold of Mr Wilson.'

At the door, he turned.

'Thanks, Staff,' he said. With difficulty, he smiled. 'I thought that anyone who could take on a dog like William would be a match for my brother!'

CHAPTER FOUR

SOON after Ross had gone, Karen saw that Adam Cameron was coming out of his drugged sleep.

He moved restlessly, hampered by the cage over the bed, and Karen came closer, trying to calm him.

And then, suddenly, his hand gripped her own.

'Damned fool, that's a white line, you can't come out——'

'Mr Cameron,' Karen said, steadily, clearly. 'It's all right, Mr Cameron, you're all right now, take it easy.'

Unexpectedly, he opened his eyes and looked directly at her, and she saw his surprise and bewilderment.

She leaned closer.

'There was an accident, Mr Cameron, but you're in hospital now.'

'I can see that,' Adam Cameron said irritably. 'I feel like hell.' And then, with an effort that she could see took almost everything he had, he tried to smile. 'Sorry, Nurse—not your fault.'

He closed his eyes, and Karen sat beside him, waiting.

'I don't remember much,' he said, after a while. 'Just that damned fool coming out and hitting me. I suppose my car's in pretty bad shape?'

For some reason this unexpected question gave Karen more problems than she would have thought. Her throat was tight.

'I don't know about your car, Mr Cameron,' she told him truthfully. 'I'll try to find out for you.'

For a long time, Adam Cameron lay with his eyes closed.

'Was Ross here?' he asked then.

'Yes, your brother was here,' Karen replied. 'Mr Cameron, you can have another injection any time, if the pain is bad. You're due for one in half an hour, but your brother said you could have it early.'

'I'll wait,' Adam Cameron said brusqely. 'But this right leg of mine must be in pretty bad shape, from the way it feels.'

Suddenly he opened his eyes and looked directly at her.

'There is something else I remember,' he said slowly. 'Someone—Ross, I think, or Frank Wilson—someone said something. I couldn't hear properly, and I thought they must have made a mistake.'

He must have seen the truth in her face. His hand gripped hers, surprisingly hard, for a moment, and then, as if all his strength had gone, he released her.

'It was Ross; I remember that now,' he said, and she could see that even speaking was an effort now. 'He told me they'd had to amputate my leg.' And then, the grey eyes pleading with her, 'I must have dreamed that, Nurse?'

She had to be honest with him; there was no kindness in putting him off, in telling him not to worry.

'I'm sorry, Mr Cameron,' she said steadily. 'Your leg was very badly crushed. It was necessary to do an amputation below the knee.'

He had lost so much blood that his face was like parchment, but now, as his eyes held hers, he seemed to become grey with the shock of this.

'Get my brother,' he said at last, tersely.

'He was here a little while ago; I think he may be in Theatre now,' Karen told him.

Adam Cameron's lips were a thin line.

'Get him here,' he said.

Karen rang the bell that connected her with Sister Baynes's office. A moment later Sister Baynes came in.

'Oh, Mr Cameron, you're with us again——' she began, but the man in the bed cut her off.

'I want to see Ross,' he told her. 'Now.'

His brusqueness didn't faze Sister Baynes.

'I'll do what I can,' she said equably. 'But you know yourself, Mr Cameron, that if he's in Theatre you'll just have to wait.'

Adam Cameron closed his eyes.

'Perhaps he should have his injection a wee bit early, Staff,' Sister Baynes said, her voice low.

'No, he will not,' the surgeon said clearly.

Sister Baynes shrugged and went out of the room. Karen checked her tray, to make sure she had the injection ready in case Ross was already operating.

Sister Baynes put her head round the door.

'He's on his way,' she said. 'I just caught him, and he can spare five minutes.'

Karen knew the sound of Ross Cameron's feet, and she could recognise the swift stride coming along the corridor. At the door, Ross stopped. His eyes met Karen's, and she knew the question he was asking. She nodded.

Ross moved closer to the bed.

'So you're with us again, Adam,' he said evenly.

His brother opened his eyes.

'Damn you, Ross,' he returned, and there was

accusation in his voice, 'surely you could have saved my leg?'

Karen saw all the colour leave Ross Cameron's face, and heard his indrawn breath.

'No, Adam, we couldn't,' he said, after a moment. 'I'm sorry about that, but we had no choice.'

'You're sorry! You're not half as sorry as I am. What kind of surgeon am I going to be with half a leg missing?'

Karen moved, feeling she should go out, for the hostility and the bitterness in Adam Cameron's voice was too private, too personal for an outsider to hear. But Ross Cameron shook his head.

He put his hand on his brother's shoulder.

'I wish we could have saved your leg, Adam.'

The man in the bed turned his head away.

'Who operated?' he asked abruptly.

It was only for a moment that Ross hesitated.

'I did,' he said, and his voice was steady. 'Frank Wilson assisted.' He turned to Karen. 'I think Mr Cameron should have his injection now, Nurse.'

'Oh, yes, put him out when he's too troublesome,' Adam said bitterly.

Karen prepared the injection, but Ross Cameron took the syringe from her, and, while she held Adam's arm steady, he pressed the plunger.

'I'll come back and see you later, Adam,' he said.

'Don't bother,' Adam returned, and already his voice was blurred. 'You've done enough, thanks.'

Karen and Ross stood beside the bed, looking down at their patient, as he gave up his effort to keep his eyes open.

'I'm sorry you had to be part of that, Nurse Taylor,'

Ross said softly, after a while. 'But there could be plenty more, so you might as well get used to it.'

She could see that he was trying very hard to be detached and professional about this, and she could see, too, how hard this was. She wished there was something she could say to help him, but there was nothing.

'I have to go,' Ross said abruptly.

At the door he turned.

'My mother will be here some time today, Nurse. Otherwise, no visitors.'

And I wonder, Karen thought, as she heard him stride off down the long corridor, when the girl with fair hair will come.

Adam Cameron was still heavily sedated later in the afternoon when Sister Baynes brought his mother in.

Mrs Cameron was obviously upset, and her dark brown eyes—so like Ross's, Karen realised—were shadowed. But in spite of her distress, and her quickly suppressed gasp when she saw the still figure in the bed, she managed to smile at Karen.

'If he's asleep, I won't disturb him, Nurse,' she said softly. 'I just had to see him for myself.'

'Sit down here, Mrs Cameron,' Karen said, and drew the chair close to the bed. 'Then he'll see you if he does wake.'

Mrs Cameron's thick white hair grew back from her forehead in the same way as Ross's did, Karen saw. Ross, in fact, was very like his mother, with the same firm jaw, the same cleft in his chin, and the same high cheekbones.

'Is he in much pain, Nurse?' Mrs Cameron asked.

There was no point in pretending, for the lines of pain were there to be seen on Adam Cameron's face.

'Yes, he is,' Karen said steadily. 'We're keeping him fairly heavily sedated, for the moment.'

She had to stay in the room, but in an effort to give the older woman some privacy with her unconscious son she took her charts over to the window and worked on them.

For a long time Mrs Cameron sat silent, with Adam's hand in hers, then Karen heard her say, softly, sadly, 'Oh, my boy, my boy!'

Karen felt her eyes blur with tears, and she couldn't pretend she hadn't heard. She moved to the bed and put one hand on the older woman's shoulder. After a moment Mrs Cameron covered it with her own.

'Would you like a cup of tea, Mrs Cameron?' Karen asked softly.

'Thank you, my dear, I would appreciate that,' Mrs Cameron said, not quite steadily.

There was a kettle in the room, and Karen made tea for both of them. Just as Mrs Cameron handed her back the empty cup, the man on the bed opened his eyes.

'Mother?' he said, and he didn't seem surprised. 'You shouldn't have come—Ross shouldn't have let you.'

'Don't be silly, Adam,' his mother said firmly. 'Why on earth not? You know very well I'd worry more about you if I didn't see you.'

'I suppose you know?' Adam said abruptly. 'About my leg?'

'Yes, I do,' his mother replied. 'It's dreadful, Adam, and I'm so sorry, but I'd rather have you alive with half a leg than dead!'

Good for you, Karen thought, in surprised admiration. So often people were afraid to mention an amputation.

'I'm not so sure about that, Mother,' said Adam, his voice low.

'I can understand that, right now,' his mother agreed, and it was only because Karen was looking at her closely that she saw the effort it took the older woman to speak steadily, evenly. 'I can only tell you how I feel.'

Suddenly she looked worn out.

'I think I'll go, Adam,' she said, and kissed her son's cheek. 'But I'll be back tomorrow—I'm staying with cousin Helen for a few days.'

Karen went to the door with her.

'Thanks for the tea, Nurse Taylor,' Mrs Cameron said, and she was in control of herself again. 'Ross said you would look after Adam well.'

It was a professional compliment, nothing more, Karen knew that, but she couldn't help feeling a warm glow of pleasure, thinking of Ross Cameron's talking about her in that way to his mother.

And it helped, to know that he had said that, when she found it heavy going, looking after a difficult, irritable patient who was in considerable pain. And who found it hard, if not impossible, to come to terms with what had happened to him.

Karen, sitting one day getting Adam Cameron's chart ready for Ross or Mr Wilson coming, looked over at the man in the bed, deeply sedated at the moment. Unconsciously, she sighed deeply.

'Are things a bit much for you, Nurse Taylor?' asked Sister Newton from the door, and the sympathy in her voice was almost too much for Karen.

She tried to smile.

'A bit,' she admitted. She straightened her shoulders. 'But I'll be fine. It's just—Sister Newton, he's so bitter, so—angry. It doesn't seem to get through to him that his brother saved his life.'

The older woman sat down in the chair beside the window.

'Of course he's bitter and angry, Nurse,' she said quietly. 'He had no time to prepare himself for this, and he's having to face it at a time when his physical condition is poor, and when he's in so much pain. Hang on to that, and it might help you.'

She stood up and went over to the bed. For a long time she stood looking down at the unconscious man, and Karen knew that what Moira had heard was true. There had been something between these two.

Sister Newton looked up, and Karen felt herself colouring, certain that the older woman knew what she was thinking.

'We were once—quite friendly, Adam and I,' she said, almost to herself. 'I'm a few years older than he is, but it didn't seem to matter. But maybe I read more into it than I should have. Anyway, we're still good friends, and we always will be. I do have that.'

She smiled, with difficulty.

'But I know very well that he will not be an easy patient, and I have every sympathy with you. Come and cry on my shoulder any time you need to.'

Once again she was brisk and professional, as she questioned Karen about Adam's progress. But when she had gone Karen knew that what the older woman had said, about Adam Cameron's difficulty in handling this without time to prepare himself for it, had undoubtedly helped her.

She was just handing over to the night nurse when Moira Sullivan beckoned from the door.

'Don't forget the party tonight,' she said.

Karen had completely forgotten that Moira and her flatmates were having a party. Her dismay must have shown on her face, for Moira shook her red-gold head.

'No, you're not getting out of it,' she said firmly. 'You need a break. Besides, I've promised Patience that you'll meet her at the gate just before eight, and bring her with you.'

And she was off, not giving Karen a chance to refuse.

'She's right, Karen,' the night nurse said. 'You look tired—a party will do you good.'

Usually there was nothing Karen liked more than a party, but tonight she felt she'd much rather just put her feet up, have supper on a tray—with William lying at, or more usually on her feet—and relax.

With reluctance, she dressed in jeans and a casual shirt, for Moira's parties always ended with those who weren't dancing sitting on the floor. No time to wash her hair, she knew, so she brushed it over her head, grabbed her coat, and apologised to William, whose mournful face and dejected ears convinced her even more that she'd much rather have been staying at home.

Patience was waiting at the gate, and she smiled when she saw what Karen was wearing.

'I didn't know just how casual Moira meant,' she said with relief. 'Is it far?'

Karen shook her head. 'Just a couple of streets.'

The other girl smiled. 'Now, when you say a couple, do you mean two, like they do here in Scotland, or do you mean more, like we do in South Africa?'

Karen laughed.

'I mean two—a Scottish couple. That was one of the things I had to get used to.'

As they walked—quickly, because it was cold—she asked Patience about her training in the huge Durban hospital, and by the time they reached Moira's flat they had discovered quite a few people they both knew, nurses who had moved between Cape Town and Durban. And already Karen was feeling much less reluctant about the party.

The room was crowded, as she had expected, and the music was loud. Patience was claimed by one of the young interns, and soon Karen saw them dancing, at the far side of the room. She herself shook her head when she was asked to dance.

'Later, thanks, Ted,' she said to the young doctor. 'I need to sit down for a bit.'

He nodded in sympathy, and went off cheerfully to find someone else to dance with.

Karen found a corner near the fire and sat down on a cushion on the floor. It wasn't that she had been on her feet much, she thought, but somehow she was very tired. She closed her eyes, grateful for the warmth, and grateful, too, for the noise, for the music, for the knowledge that she was here with friends.

'I didn't expect to see you here,' a voice very close to her said.

She opened her eyes and looked right into Ross Cameron's dark brown eyes.

'And I certainly didn't expect to see you,' she said, with truth. 'I would have got out of it if I could, but Moira insisted.'

'Moira—oh, yes, the Irish redhead, Ian's girl. It was Ian who made me come—said it would do me good,' Ross told her.

He sat down on the floor beside her.

'I think he was right too,' he went on. 'And I bet you need a break.'

He looked down at her.

'I don't know what your first name is,' he said abruptly.

'Karen,' she told him.

'Until now, you've been Staff Nurse Taylor, or William's mistress,' he said, and held out his hand. 'Hi, Karen. And I suppose you know that I'm Ross.'

His hand was firm and warm on hers. Not a big hand, she had noticed before, for a good surgeon needed hands that weren't too big.

'Do you want to dance, or do you want to eat?' he asked her, and she realised that he intended staying with her.

'Eat, I think,' she said, a little faintly.

He took her hand and helped her to her feet. With both her hands still in his, he looked down at her. 'Tonight,' he told her firmly, 'we're not going to talk about the hospital, or about my brother. Agreed?'

'Agreed,' she said, and followed him through to the kitchen, where there was a large pot of risotto on the stove, and a large bowl of salad on the table.

Ross poured wine for both of them, and they took their plates of food back to the tiny corner of the floor where Karen had been sitting. It was really too noisy for much talking, and in a way she was glad of that, for, in spite of what he had said, it was difficult not to speak about the only things they had in common—the hospital, and his brother.

Later they danced, as far as it was possible to dance in the crowded room. Quite unlike the other time they had danced together, Karen couldn't help thinking, when she was in her rose-pink dress, at the Hospital

Ball. But Ross didn't realise that the girl he had danced with that night—in anger, because his brother had claimed the girl with fair hair—was the girl he was dancing with now.

Abruptly, Ross stopped dancing.

'I've had enough,' he said, looking down at her. 'Do you want to stay, or can I take you home? I presume you live fairly close.'

'At the far side of the Gardens,' she told him. She could feel colour rising in her cheeks. 'But you don't have to take me home; I'm quite capable of walking on my own.'

He smiled, and the warmth of his smile took away the abruptness of the way he had spoken.

'I'd like to, Karen,' he said.

The gates of the park were locked, so they had to walk round the side. It was a clear, cold night, and the stars were bright in the autumn sky.

'Where did you get William?' Ross asked, looking down at her.

'There was a notice on the board in the canteen, soon after I got here,' Karen told him. 'Labrador pups for sale. We'd always had a Labrador at home, and—well, I was a little homesick at first; I couldn't replace my family, but I thought having a dog would help.'

'And it does?' he asked, as if he really wanted to know.

'Oh, yes,' Karen replied. 'William is very good company.'

'I can imagine,' said Ross, and there was laughter in his voice. 'He's quite a dog!'

They had reached the steps that led down to her basement flat.

'This is where I live,' Karen said, and all at once she was a little breathless.

Ross looked down at her.

'You look quite different, out of uniform,' he said, a little awkwardly.

I should move away, Karen thought. I should just say goodnight, and walk down the steps.

But she didn't.

'It's late,' she said, and she knew her voice was unsteady.

'I know,' he agreed.

Gently, with one finger, he traced the outline of her lips.

'Goodnight, Karen,' he said softly.

He kissed her, his lips warm on hers, gentle at first, and then not at all gentle.

CHAPTER FIVE

It was a long time before Ross released her.

'I didn't mean to do that,' he said abruptly. But not apologising, and Karen was glad of that.

'It's all right,' she replied. And then, as lightly as she could—and that was far from easy, with her heart thudding unsteadily, 'A goodnight kiss is a nice way to finish an evening, after all, Ross.'

And to prove that she meant that, she stood on tiptoe and kissed him fleetingly.

'Goodnight,' she said. 'And thanks for walking me home.'

She went inside quickly, and closed the door to prevent William rushing out and greeting Ross. When she had given him a biscuit and patted him, she sat down.

I didn't mean to do that, he had said. And she had said it was all right.

And it was, because she was not, she told herself sensibly and firmly, going to make anything at all out of one kiss. Like that time at the Ball, she'd just happened to be there.

And yet—what was that song her mother was so fond of, an old song? Something about giving me a kiss to build a dream on.

No, sir, Karen told herself. I am not building any dreams on one kiss from you, Ross Cameron. And you needn't be afraid it will affect our professional relationship.

55

She should have known, of course, that Ross himself would be conscious of that, and when he greeted her the next day, in Adam's room, he was completely professional.

'Morning, Nurse Taylor. Morning, Adam. Charts, please, Nurse.'

He examined his brother's wound then, Karen taking the bandage off. All the time he did this Adam Cameron lay still and stiff, unresponsive.

'Healing nicely,' Ross murmured. He straightened. 'Adam, I want you to start physiotherapy. I'll arrange it with the physio department, and Nurse Taylor can take you along once a day.'

'And that will be a sight for St Margaret's,' Adam returned, 'a senior surgeon being pushed along in a wheelchair like a baby!'

Ross sat down on the edge of the bed.

'It won't be very pleasant, I know that, Adam,' he said quietly. 'But it has to be done.'

'Character-building,' Adam returned. And, taking Karen completely by surprise, both men laughed.

'Something our mother used to tell us when we were children,' Adam explained, 'when we had to do something particularly unpleasant.' He took a deep breath. 'Ross, Frank Wilson was talking to me yesterday. He told me that if he'd had his way a complete amputation would have been done, but you insisted that you could make it just a lower limb job. I'm—grateful for that.'

It must have been very hard for him to say that, Karen knew, for she had seen that he was not a man who could apologise easily. And this was as close to an apology as he could come.

'I wish I could have done more,' Ross said, his voice low.

He turned to Karen.

'We can do away with the sandbags now, Nurse Taylor. I want you to get my brother into a prone position for half an hour at a time, maybe twice a day to start with.' He looked at his brother. 'You know all about adducting and extending the stump, Adam, to exercise the adductor and gluteal muscles.'

'You forgot to tell her to pinch a pillow between my thighs,' Adam Cameron said flatly, and Karen could see that the momentary warmth between the two men had gone.

'I was just going to,' Ross replied tightly. 'And before you think I've forgotten anything else, you'll be having infra-red irradiation to improve circulation, and you'll also be measured for crutches.'

But the older surgeon hadn't finished.

'And you can cut down that analgesic dosage,' he said. 'I can do with less, and I don't like being knocked out.'

Karen, looking at Ross, saw the anger that had been there leave his face.

'You've needed it, Adam,' he said quietly. 'But we'll reduce it, if you want.'

He made the adjustment on the chart and handed it to Karen.

'Oh, Nurse Taylor,' he said, 'thanks for reminding me the other day about my promise to young Jenny—I've managed to persuade Sister Baynes to have someone take the young fellow through to visit her this afternoon. I'll have a word with Sister on the way out—maybe someone could relieve you for five minutes, and let you see those kids meeting.'

He was as good as his word, and an hour later Sister

Baynes herself came to take over in Adam Cameron's room.

'I believe the girl was a special patient of yours, Nurse Taylor,' she said, settling herself in the chair beside the window. 'And it will do this young lad the world of good; he's been feeling very bad about what happened to her.'

Young Bob didn't look any older than Jenny. Too young, Karen thought indignantly, to be in charge of a powerful machine, and two lives. But she could see from the shadows in the boy's grey eyes that he had been carrying a load of guilt about Jenny.

When Karen and the nurse pushing the wheelchair reached the door of Women's Surgical, Karen saw, with pleasure, that Jenny was sitting up now, and the bandage on her head was smaller.

'Hello, Jenny,' the boy said, as they reached Jenny's bed.

''Lo, Bob,' Jenny said, her voice very casual. 'How're you feeling?'

'A lot better,' Bob said. 'How about you?'

'I'm going home next week,' Jenny told him.

There was a long silence.

'I'm sorry they had to cut your bonny hair,' Bob said, in a burst.

Jenny's face clouded, but only for a moment.

'It's starting to grow already,' she told him. And then, cheekily, 'I might have guessed you'd get yourself one of the pretty nurses!'

The nurse who had brought him in the wheelchair laughed.

'I'll leave you to do your own explaining, Bob.' She looked at her fob watch. 'Ten minutes, you can have, then I'll be back to take you for physio.'

'Nurse,' Jenny said, suddenly shy. 'You too, Nurse Taylor—thanks a lot, for bringing Bob.'

'Young love,' the other nurse said, as she and Karen went out of the ward. 'I think they'll get on much better without us there, don't you?'

Karen agreed.

'Back to your patient,' the dark-haired girl said sympathetically. 'I don't envy you; it can't be easy looking after Adam Cameron.'

No, it isn't, Karen thought, as she went back to the small side-ward. Ross had been right; Adam Cameron would often tell her how things should be done, and he was very demanding, but she kept reminding herself of what Sister Newton had said. Adam had had no chance, no time, to get used to the idea of this amputation. He was having to come to terms with it while he was having so much pain, so much discomfort, and that must be very hard.

'Your physiotherapy is arranged for tomorrow morning, Mr Cameron,' she told him a little later, when a message was brought to her.

'And after that, what about some occupational therapy?' Adam suggested. 'I could learn to make baskets, or trays.'

Karen looked at him.

'I don't think anyone is suggesting the need for that, Mr Cameron,' she said cautiously.

'I'm surprised, then,' he shot back, and his voice was bitter. 'What else am I to do? I can't be much of a surgeon with half a leg missing!'

'You'll be fitted with a prosthesis, Mr Cameron,' Karen pointed out.

'I know, and it will be so good that people will hardly know,' he said drily. 'But let me tell you, Nurse Taylor, you can be damned sure that no matter how good the prosthesis is it will not be a real leg, and I will not be able to balance on it to do surgery!'

It was so unfortunate, Karen thought later, that it was then, with Adam Cameron in that mood of bitterness and anger, that Ross came in.

While Karen was trying to think of the right words to say, the words that would not just be empty reassurance, she heard Ross's footsteps. Ross's, and someone else.

'I've brought you a visitor, Adam,' said Ross, and he ushered in the fair-haired girl. Her blue eyes were wide and anxious, as she went a little nearer to the bed.

'Oh, Adam,' she said unsteadily, 'I wanted to come before, but Ross said I'd have to wait.'

She bent over the man in the bed and kissed him. Adam Cameron made no move to hold her closer to him, and there was no softening of the lines of bitterness on his face.

'So Ross has been keeping you in touch with the patient's progress, has he?' he asked.

Her fair head still close to him, the girl nodded.

'I would have come right away, but he said to wait,' she murmured.

Above her head, Adam Cameron's grey eyes met his brother's.

'You didn't waste any time, did you?' he said. 'Just the chance you've been waiting for.'

Karen saw the colour drain from Ross's face at the hostility in Adam's voice.

'You have no right to say that, Adam,' he returned, his voice low.

The girl looked from one to the other, upset, confused. Karen couldn't help feeling sorry for her.

'Shona, I'm sure hospital visiting isn't really in your line, now is it, lass?' Adam said, his voice falsely bright.

Colour flooded the girl's cheeks.

'Don't say that, Adam. This isn't hospital visiting, this is me coming to see you! I—I'd come to see you anywhere.'

For a moment Adam looked at her, and Karen thought he made an involuntary movement, as if he would have held her close to him. But he stopped himself.

'I'm sorry, but I'm not really in the mood for visitors today,' he said brusquely. 'Maybe some other time.' He turned to Karen. 'I think I'll have my injection now, Nurse.'

Shona Macdonald stood up.

'I didn't think you'd be looking on me as a visitor, Adam,' she said, and there was a pathetic dignity in her face. 'I'll go now. No, Ross, I'll get the bus home.'

She went out of the room, her fair head held high. But Karen had seen how close to tears she was.

'That was unforgivable, Adam!' Ross snapped. 'You must have seen how much you were hurting Shona.'

Adam closed his eyes.

'The sooner Shona realises that everything has changed, the better for all of us,' he said. 'I would have thought you would be the first to realise that, Ross. Nurse Taylor, you can give me my injection now.'

'Adam——' Ross began, but Adam interrupted him.

'My injection, Nurse.'

His face was grey and drawn, and he was clearly in pain. Without a word, Karen prepared his injection and gave it to him. It was quick in action, and within a few moments he was asleep.

Karen, occupied with adjusting his position, making sure he was as comfortable as possible, thought Ross had gone. But when she turned round he was standing at the window, looking out.

'Mr Cameron——' she began hesitantly.

He swung round.

'He had no right to say that,' he said bleakly. 'He must know I couldn't think——'

It was not at all professional, and she might regret it later, but Karen put one hand on his arm.

'Sit down,' she told him. 'I'll make you a cup of tea—I think you could do with it.'

He sat in silence while she made tea. But when she handed him a mug, he tried to smile.

'No wonder you and my mother got on well together! She thinks a cup of tea can put anything right.'

'I wouldn't just say that,' Karen replied, relieved to see that some of the colour had returned to his face, and some of the hurt had gone. 'But I do think it helps.'

She sat down on the other chair, not saying anything, seeing that Ross needed this silence.

'When we were wee boys, the two of us,' Ross said unexpectedly, 'I thought the world of my big brother. He's six years older than me, and he was always the leader—whatever Adam said I was to do, I did it. Mum used to say that if Adam told me to put my hand in a fire I would do it.'

He looked at his mug, empty now. Without a word, Karen got up and refilled it.

'Adam was eighteen when our father died, and I was twelve,' he went on, and his voice was far away. 'He became the man of the family right away; he made the decisions. Not that there was any decision to be made, ever, about the two of us doing medicine. Dad was a doctor, and his father before him, and I can't remember a time when Adam and I didn't know we would do the same.'

He was quiet again, remembering, and Karen waited.

'But surgery, now, that was another thing. I think at first Adam was pleased that I wanted to be a surgeon too, but later—I'm not so sure.'

'It can't have been easy,' Karen said carefully, 'both of you surgeons in the same hospital, and in the same team.'

Ross smiled, a smile that didn't reach his dark brown eyes.

'You could say that, right enough,' he replied. 'Maybe it would have been better if I'd gone to another hospital, but I never dreamed we would come to being—rivals, almost.'

When he had said it, he looked at her.

'I've never said that before,' he said, and there was surprise in his voice. 'I've never even thought it before, at least not consciously. I just told myself that we didn't get on so well, as grown men, as we did when we were laddies.'

He put his mug down.

'And recently, of course, there was Shona.'

He seemed to be waiting for her to say something, Karen realised.

'She's—very pretty,' she said, meaning it.

'She is that,' Ross agreed. 'She comes from the Highlands, and there's something fey about her. That's a word you'll not know, I suppose. It means—other-worldly, sort of.'

'I do know the word,' Karen told him. 'My grand-mother came from Edinburgh.'

'I think it's because of Shona that this—rivalry, this distance between us, has become greater,' Ross said then. 'I wouldn't want you to think badly of Shona——'

And why should it matter to you what I think of anyone, Karen thought, when you look like that just speaking about her, just thinking about her?

'Why should I think badly of her?' she asked.

He shrugged.

'I thought it was pretty common hospital talk that she couldn't make up her mind which Cameron brother she wanted,' he said evenly. 'But she seemed to have made up her mind when she said she'd go to the Hospital Ball with Adam. It certainly looked as if she'd chosen him.'

Karen took a deep breath. It was only a small thing, but all at once she had to bring it into the open.

'You were dancing with her,' she said clearly, 'and Adam interrupted, and—claimed her, I suppose. You walked off the floor, and you were very angry. And you asked me to dance.'

Now she had his full attention.

'It was you!' he exclaimed astonished. 'But you looked so different, when you were in a tracksuit, with your ridiculous dog. And in jeans, at that party—I'm sorry, Karen, I really am.'

She didn't think he had noticed his own slip, using her name.

'You were too angry to notice,' she explained.

Ross sighed. 'Yes, I was,' he agreed.

He looked over at the unconscious man in the bed.

'How could he think that I would take advantage of what has happened to him?' he said, his voice low. 'It was different before; we were on equal terms. I didn't even take Shona's choice that night as valid. I certainly wasn't going to stand by and let Adam win.'

He stood up. 'Of course,' he said evenly, 'everything has changed now.'

And Karen, her heart heavy, knew very well what he meant.

Before, he would have fought for Shona Macdonald; he would have challenged his brother. Now, because Adam lay helpless in bed, Ross would not in any way take advantage of this.

But that didn't change the fact that he was in love with his brother's girl.

CHAPTER SIX

'YOU'RE too easy to talk to, Karen,' Ross Cameron said, looking down at her. 'I have no right to burden you with all this.'

'I'm glad you feel you can talk to me,' Karen replied, meaning it, in spite of the heartache of hearing his talk about Shona Macdonald in the way he had. 'I think you needed to talk to someone.'

'I did,' the young surgeon admitted. 'More than I realised. Our mother knows there are problems between Adam and me, but it would hurt her to know the extent.' He smiled, with difficulty. 'She's not too keen on Shona either—firstly, I suppose, because she's an artist, but mostly because she has the idea that Shona rather enjoyed having the attentions of both the older Cameron and the younger.'

He walked over to the bed and looked down at the unconscious man.

'I don't know how this is all going to work out,' he said wearily, after a while.

Karen hesitated, then told him what Adam had said about learning to weave baskets, because he wouldn't be able to do surgery.

'That's something we'll have to think about,' Ross said. 'I don't know the answer, until I know how Adam's going to cope with his prosthesis—both physically and emotionally.'

'Well,' Karen said practically, 'the first step towards that is the physiotherapy he'll be starting tomorrow.'

Ross smiled, and now the smile reached his eyes.

'Do you know something?' he said. 'You're very good for me, Karen Taylor.'

But not very good for myself, Karen thought ruefully after he had gone, when a few words like that can mean so much to me. Too much.

As she had expected, Adam hated being put in a wheelchair and pushed along the corridor, down in the lift, and along another long corridor to the physiotherapy department. He sat in the wheelchair with both hands gripping the sides, staring straight ahead of him, nodding curtly when he was forced to return a greeting.

'This will give everyone plenty to talk about,' he said to Karen, when they were returning to their own floor. 'Did you see the great Adam Cameron, being pushed along by a wee nurse, like a bairn in a pram?'

In the lift, Karen looked down at him.

'You're a bit big for a bairn in a pram, you know,' she pointed out to him. 'And I'm not that wee. And in all honesty, Mr Cameron, I think everyone has plenty more to think about, other than being pleased to see that you're making progress.'

'Making progress!' Adam returned derisively. 'Doing my exercises, having some irradiation treatment—you call that progress?'

Karen pushed the wheelchair out of the lift and along the corridor.

'Yes, I do,' she told him firmly. 'And it's time you began to do the same.'

For a moment she thought she had gone too far. The doctor's grey eyes grew dark, and she could see the thunder gathering on his face. And then, taking her by surprise, he threw back his head and laughed.

'You may be wee, Nurse Taylor,' he said, 'but you're tough!'

Delighted, she smiled down at him.

'Maybe you're just beginning to find out how tough,' she told him.

The next day he complained less when she took him for his treatment in the physiotherapy department, although she could see that he still hated being taken in the wheelchair along the hospital corridors.

Soon after Sister Baynes had helped her to get Adam back into bed, his mother came for her daily visit.

She was a good visitor, Karen often thought. She would sit companionably beside Adam, talking if he felt like talking, quiet if he seemed to prefer that. Telling him, sometimes, little stories about the cousin she was staying with, about neighbours at home. But she was understanding, and Karen knew that, although Adam often said to her that it was ridiculous for her to stay on in Edinburgh, that she should go home, her visits meant a great deal to him.

Sometimes, when Karen went to the door with Mrs Cameron, she could see that the older woman was close to tears, that the bright and positive front was not as easily maintained as it looked. But she could see, too, that Mrs Cameron would keep her grief for her son until she was away from the hospital.

Adam Cameron's crutches had arrived, and he had had one or two sessions with the physiotherapist learning how to cope with the three-point crutch walk, how to exert pressure on his hands, and how to keep his trunk upright.

'How long before you fit me with a prosthesis?' he asked Ross abruptly one day. For a moment, Ross's eyes met Karen's, for until now he had not even been willing to discuss this.

'I'm hoping we can start with a temporary one next week,' he replied evenly. 'As you know, it may take a few months before your proper one can be fitted, but from the time you get a temporary one I want you to use the wheelchair as little as possible.

'That suits me,' Adam returned. 'And I'm sure our wee Nurse Taylor will be pleased too.'

'I'm always pleased when my patients make progress,' Karen said demurely.

There was a glint in Adam's grey eyes.

'Especially one as difficult as this one?' he asked.

Karen shook her head.

'Now what do you expect me to say to that, Mr Cameron?' she asked him.

Adam turned to Ross.

'Did you know this lassie's grandmother trained here at St Margaret's? Then she nursed a South African soldier, and went out to live in Cape Town. And Nurse Taylor was determined that she would come and work in St Margaret's too. And look what she lands for— nursing me.'

This time Karen couldn't resist a response. 'My gran did say I would find plenty of challenges, nursing at St Margaret's,' she said.

These times when there was no friction between Adam and Ross, when she could see the closeness they had had as boys, meant a great deal to her. Mostly, she knew all too well, because she could see how much they meant to Ross. She hoped he could hold on to this warmth, this closeness, later that day, when Adam was once again bitter and hostile, saying he was sure, from all he heard, that everyone on the surgical team looked on the younger Mr Cameron as a great success.

'And how would you ever have got a chance like this, Ross, if I hadn't been lying here?' he asked. 'For you and I both know fine that I was standing in your way. I hear you made a good job of that gastro-intestinal decompression.'

'I hope I did,' Ross replied. His voice was calm and level, but Karen saw that his knuckles were white. 'Do you want to hear about it? It was quite interesting.'

Adam turned his head away. 'No, I do not want to hear about it,' he said flatly. 'In fact, I'm sorry I mentioned it.'

That set the pattern for the rest of the day, and Karen was only too glad to hand over to the night nurse, and to come off duty at five. She was glad when she was off at this time, for it was still light enough to take William into the Gardens.

She had just crossed the road from the hospital gate when a tall figure came towards her.

'Karen?' Ross Cameron said. 'I checked the off-duty list, and I saw you were coming off now. I was hoping you would be thinking of taking the Hound of the Baskervilles for a run.'

'Yes, I was,' Karen replied, and wondered if her pleasure was all too clear to see, for he was smiling now as he looked down at her.

'Would William mind some company?' he asked. 'I need some fresh air, and some exercise, and—well, I need company, Karen.'

'William will be delighted,' Karen replied.

She had to walk quickly, to keep up with Ross's long strides. He had already changed into a tracksuit and trainers.

At her door, she paused. They could both hear William's yelps of welcome from inside.

'He'll be very pleased to see you,' she warned Ross, as she turned the key in the lock.

William shot out, large and black and enthusiastic. He greeted Karen with two paws on her shoulders, and a quick look into her face, as if to reassure himself that she had survived the day without him. Then he discovered Ross. With a bark of joy he launched himself at this new friend, but fortunately Ross had had time to brace himself.

'Does this happen every day?' he asked Karen breathlessly. 'Down, you dope!'

William sat down, and offered Ross a large black paw. Solemnly, Ross shook it.

'He'll just go on and on; he doesn't know when to stop,' said Karen. 'Yes, I get this welcome every time I come in, as if I'd been away for years. Ross, I'd like to change—I'll only be a couple of minutes.'

She hurried through to the tiny bedroom, and threw her uniform off and her tracksuit on. When she got back, Ross was sitting down, and William was still offering him a paw.

'Walk, William,' Karen said, and with one short bark of delight William bounded to the back door, where his lead hung.

'I'll take him,' Ross offered. 'I don't know how you manage.'

'I don't know either,' Karen admitted. 'I just hang on, and wait for the middle, where I can let him off.'

William's ball was in her pocket, and, to William's delight, Ross threw it much further for him.

'Takes him longer to get back,' Ross said with

satisfaction. 'We can gather our strength together— oh, here he comes.'

William, ball in mouth, skidded to a halt at their feet, dropped the ball, and looked up at Ross expectantly.

'Once more,' Ross told him firmly.

Next time he put the ball in his pocket, and put William on the lead.

'I must admit it's nice just to walk back, instead of being pulled,' Karen said, for William seemed to accept Ross's authority. 'He's walking just like any ordinary dog.'

'He doesn't accept you as a top dog,' Ross told her, as they crossed the road. 'I've had plenty of big dogs, and you always have to let them know that you're the top dog, the boss, not them.'

'I think William has already decided that I belong to him, rather than him to me,' Karen admitted. They were at the steps leading down to her door. Ross had asked if he could come with them, but perhaps that was as far as he wanted it to go. On the other hand, the rain had just started.

'Would you like to come in?' she asked him.

'Thanks, I would,' he said.

When the door was closed behind them, he looked around.

'It's an interesting little flat,' he remarked.

'It's all I could afford,' Karen told him honestly. 'And it does have a tiny garden at the back, so in summer I can leave the door open, and William can get out.'

She looked at him.

'I was going to have an omelette and some salad,' she said hesitantly. 'Would you like to join me?'

'If you don't mind, I'd like that very much,' said Ross. 'I wasn't enjoying my own company too much, I must admit. Which are you better at, the omelette or the salad? Because I'm pretty good at omelettes.'

'Fine, then I'll make a salad,' Karen replied.

Sometimes Moira came for a meal, and they got things ready together, but Karen had to admit that, in spite of vague sympathies for Women's Lib, vague feelings that friends were friends, whatever—this was different. It was fun—it was a lot of fun. And Ross was right; he was good at making omelettes. And at washing up.

'I have enjoyed this,' he said, at the door, much later.

'So have I,' Karen replied.

He looked down at her. Afterwards, she was certain that he hadn't intended kissing her. But the next moment his arms were around her, and his lips on hers, and after the warmth and the sharing of the past hours it seemed natural and right.

Slowly, Ross let her go.

'This seems to be becoming a habit,' he said, and her heart turned over, because his voice wasn't quite steady. 'Look, Karen, I don't know what you must think, after some of the things I've told you——'

'About Shona Macdonald?' Karen said steadily. 'Ross, as long as you're not—cheating on her, in any way, then it's all right with me.'

'Oh, I'm not cheating on Shona,' he replied. 'In all fairness, right from the start she seemed to prefer Adam. But there was always a chance for me, and even after she decided to go to the Hospital Ball with him I wasn't prepared to give up.'

His dark eyes were troubled now.

'I would have gone on fighting for her,' he said abruptly. 'But I cannot and will not fight a man who's just been crippled, a man whose whole life has been changed—and that man my brother, what's more.'

He took both her hands in his.

'But at the same time, perhaps it's not right or fair that I should be kissing you, Karen, unless you know this?'

Karen laughed lightly, and, as she did, she wondered if Ross could know just how hard this was for her.

'Ross, I think you're putting far too much on a kiss or two. You enjoyed it—I enjoyed it—do we really need to do all this soul-searching?'

She wasn't sure, afterwards, if there was relief or some disappointment in his dark brown eyes.

'You're right, of course,' he said, after a moment. 'As your grandmother would probably tell you, we Scots do have a tendency to think a bit too much!'

But when he had gone she couldn't help wondering how wise she was, for perhaps it would be better to cut off any further involvement with Ross Cameron right now, before she got hurt.

It was the day after that that Shona Macdonald came back to see Adam.

Karen, talking to Adam's mother, saw that Mrs Cameron was looking beyond her, at the doorway, and she turned round. Shona Macdonald stood there, her blue eyes anxious, her cheeks flushed.

'I'm sorry,' she said hesitantly. 'I didn't know—I'll come some other time.'

Mrs Cameron stood up.

'Hello, Shona,' she said coolly. 'I was just going, anyway.'

'You don't have to go, Mum,' Adam said.

But his mother kissed him, picked up her handbag, and went, promising to come again the next day.

'I brought you some grapes, Adam,' Shona said awkwardly.

'Thanks, that was nice of you,' Adam replied.

Karen pulled out the chair Mrs Cameron had been sitting on.

'Sit down, won't you?' she said.

The fair-haired girl sat down. Karen wished she could go out and leave them alone, but she had to stay with her patient. She carried her charts over to the chair beside the window, and worked, quite unnecessarily, on them.

'Adam,' Shona said, her voice low, 'don't shut me out like this; don't send me away.'

'Have some sense, Shona!' Adam said roughly. 'You must realise this has changed everything.'

'Why should it do that, Adam?' Shona asked. 'It doesn't change the way we feel about each other.'

'Listen to me,' said Adam. 'You and I had fun together, we danced, we played tennis, we walked on the beach. I was a successful surgeon, with a very promising career ahead of me. Now, I don't know what I'm going to do, but I do know there'll not be much in the way of dancing and walking and playing games.'

'None of that matters, Adam,' Shona said unsteadily. 'All that—it's just things to do. We can do different things—it doesn't matter, as long as we're together.'

'Stop it, Shona,' Adam told her. 'Stop it before you say something you might regret. You don't want to spend the rest of your life with a cripple.'

'Adam——' the girl began, but he broke in.

'And I don't want anyone's pity,' he told her. 'I

don't want to be hampered and tied by the weight of your feeling sorry for me, Shona.' He laughed, and there was so much bitterness in his laughter that Karen's heart ached. 'I'm just sorry I hadn't got around to giving you a ring, because then you could have given it back to me, and that would have put a satisfactory line under the whole thing. As it is, let's just say we'll call it a day. You get on with your life, and I'll get on with what's left of mine.'

Karen heard the girl's indrawn breath.

'Is that what you want, Adam?' she asked unsteadily.

'That's what I want,' Adam replied.

Without a word, Shona got up and went out of the room.

And Karen could not keep silent any longer.

'Did you have to do that, Mr Cameron?' she said, going over to him.

'Of course I had to,' Adam returned. 'She's soft-hearted, you can see that, and she would have stuck with me, and——' He turned his head away. 'And although I may have to live with only half a leg, I cannot and will not live with Shona's pity,' he said, his voice low.

'But are you sure——?' Karen began.

But he would not discuss it any further.

'Surely it's time for me to do my exercises, is it not, Nurse Taylor? I wouldn't want you to be in trouble with my brother, through not obeying your instructions.'

Karen had to give up then.

But the whole sad episode would not leave her, and later, when she was in the staff-room having tea, Moira Sullivan sat down beside her, and noticed immediately that something was bothering her.

'Is your specialling getting a bit much for you?' she asked sympathetically.

Karen nodded.

'It is, a bit,' she admitted. She couldn't, of course, tell Moira or anyone else that Adam had sent Shona Macdonald away, and so she said only that it was understandably difficult for Adam to adjust, to handle this devastating thing that had happened to him.

'He's very bitter, sometimes,' she said. 'I can understand that, but it's hard to take.'

Moira's blue eyes were warm.

'It's very demanding,' she agreed, 'having a special patient, and it's very difficult not to get—more involved than you want to be.' She hesitated. 'He's quite a fellow, is Adam Cameron. You sure you're not falling in love with him, Karen?'

Startled, Karen put her cup down.

'Oh, no, Moira,' she said with certainty. 'I'm not at all likely to fall in love with Adam Cameron.'

Slow understanding dawned in the Irish girl's eyes.

'Then it's Ross,' she said. 'You're in love with Ross.'

CHAPTER SEVEN

THERE was little point in Karen's denying it, for she knew the warm tide of colour in her face had given her away.

'I wondered, that night of the party,' Moira told her. 'But I did think it must be just because of your nursing Adam that you and Ross spent so much time together. Because of course——' She stopped.

'Because of course he's in love with Shona Macdonald too,' Karen finished for her. 'That's what you were going to say, isn't it, Moira?'

Moira nodded.

'Yes, I was,' she agreed. She hesitated, but only for a moment. 'Does this change anything, this accident of Adam's—for all of them?'

'I don't know,' Karen said honestly. She could not, of course, tell Moira about the scene she had been forced to overhear, about Adam Cameron's determination that he did not want pity from Shona.

'It might force this girl to make up her mind once and for all, between the two of them,' Moira said thoughtfully.

And if she did, if she took Adam at his word, then that left the way wide open for Ross and her. Apart from Ross's scruples about taking his chance with his brother crippled. But how would Ross feel when he knew it was Adam's decision?

Karen stood up and pushed her chair back.

'It isn't my problem,' she said with decision. 'Because of course Ross has no idea how I feel.'

Moira's blue eyes were clear and candid.

'Isn't it?' she asked.

No, of course it isn't, Karen told herself, and she reminded herself of the old song she had thought of about a kiss to build a dream on. No sensible girl would ever build a dream on the kisses she and Ross Cameron had had.

And I am, she told herself, a sensible girl. It was very pleasant, being kissed by Ross Cameron—very pleasant indeed, she thought, and her treacherous heart turned over at the memory of just how pleasant it was—but she had to regard these kisses as just that, a pleasant and logical conclusion to times together.

And, having settled all that in her mind, Karen went back to her patient, who was in an even worse mood than usual, so that she needed all her reserves of patience and professionalism to deal with him.

'It's time this nonsense of being specialled stopped,' Adam told her abruptly, as she was changing his bandage.

'You know very well, Mr Cameron,' Karen reminded him, as she washed and powdered his wound, 'that Mr Wilson believes there's still a danger of possible hae-morrhage. He and your brother feel you still need a nurse with you constantly.'

'I'm fed up with nurses and hospitals,' Adam muttered, staring up at the roof while she finished his bandage and put on the clean woollen stump sock that had to be changed every day. 'Believe me, Nurse Taylor, I never realised how little privacy patients had.'

Karen stood back and looked down at him.

'I'm sorry about that, Mr Cameron,' she said steadily. 'I have as little wish as you to intrude on your privacy. But I have my orders. And perhaps the experience of being a patient will add to your understanding as a doctor.'

'Nurse Taylor,' said Adam, and his voice was tight, 'I think I've had enough of the sweetness and light for today.'

And in spite of all Karen's resolutions to keep what Sister Newton had said in her mind, to remember that Adam had had no chance to prepare himself for the shock of this before it happened, she couldn't help feeling a stab of hurt.

'I'm sorry, Mr Cameron,' she replied, as steadily as she could. 'I think I hear the supper trolley in the corridor—I'll raise the top of your bed.'

As she helped him into a sitting position, she found his grey eyes resting on her. And then, as the trolley stopped at the door, he said, abruptly, 'Sorry, Nurse.'

Karen smiled, touched more than she would have thought possible, for Adam Cameron was a man who found it very difficult to apologise.

'It's all right, Mr Cameron,' she said.

And because he had managed to say that he was sorry, she was feeling much better as she went off duty and hurried out of the hospital gate, her cloak swinging.

'Nurse Taylor?'

Startled, Karen swung round.

Shona Macdonald stood there, just outside the gate.

'I—I was waiting for you. I wanted to talk to you,' she said hesitantly. 'Could we go and have a cup of coffee somewhere?'

It was the last thing Karen wanted, any further

emotional involvement with this girl—and, she thought, with the whole Cameron family! But Shona Macdonald's heart-shaped face was drawn, and her blue eyes were shadowed. And Karen didn't have the heart to make some excuse, to say that she didn't have time.

'I live at the other side of the park,' she said resignedly. 'I have to get home, because I have a dog, and he's been on his own all day. Come with me, and we'll have coffee there.'

Shona said nothing as they walked across the park. Her hands were thrust deep in the pockets of her anorak, and her fair head was bent. She did smile when William came bounding out, and somehow William had the sense to be a little less boisterous than he usually was.

'Be careful,' warned Karen, 'he can knock you over with his welcome.'

'I'm stronger than I look,' said Shona, following her in.

She sat down docilely, like a good child, when Karen told her to, and handed Karen her anorak.

'Thanks,' she said, when Karen gave her a mug of coffee. 'I can't call you Nurse Taylor—what's your name? Karen. And you know mine is Shona?'

Now that she was here, she didn't seem to know what she wanted to say.

'I don't really know what I'm doing wasting your time,' she said at last. 'But I did need to talk to someone, and——'

She took a deep breath.

'Did Adam really mean what he said?' she asked unsteadily. 'Does he really want everything to finish between us?'

Karen thought of Adam Cameron's telling her that although he had to live with only half a leg he would not live with this girl's pity.

'Adam Cameron is a very proud man, Shona,' she said carefully. 'He's very much afraid of anyone's pitying him.'

'I love him,' Shona said, her fair head bent. 'He should know that.'

It wasn't easy to find the right words, but Karen knew she had to.

'I think he's afraid you'll feel—bound to him, because of this,' she said slowly. 'Can you really and honestly say you're not just sorry for him, Shona?'

Shona lifted her head.

'Of course I'm sorry for him!' she returned indignantly. 'Anyone would be, after what's happened to him. But it's more than that, much more. Karen, I can't imagine the rest of my life without Adam.'

Her blue eyes were steady. Karen longed just to leave it there, but this girl had asked for her help, and she owed it to her to help her to face things clear-sightedly.

'And you can imagine the rest of your life with him?' she asked. 'He's bitter and frustrated because he's crippled; he doesn't know what direction his professional life can take now—he'll be very difficult to live with. You'll have to be very sure, before you take that on.'

Shona put her empty mug down. William, as if knowing that she needed sympathy, put his head on her knee, and she rubbed his ears absently.

'I'll have to be doing some thinking,' she said, and her voice was low. She tried to smile. 'Karen, thank you for helping me to see all this. I'll go now.'

Karen walked to the top of the basement steps with her.

'If I need to talk to you again, can I get in touch with you?' asked Shona. The lamplight shone on her long fair hair, and her blue eyes held Karen's hopefully, trustingly.

I didn't want to get any more involved, Karen thought, half resenting this demand. But she could not refuse.

'Of course,' she said.

She stood watching Shona's slight figure walking away, hands thrust in her pockets again. But her fair head was held a little higher now, and somehow she seemed less hopeless than she had been.

Karen sighed, and went back down to give William his supper.

In some ways, nursing Adam Cameron was even harder now that he was recovering.

He was bored and restless, refusing point-blank to take part in any of the activities available in the day-room. It was only necessary now for Karen to use the wheelchair to take him for his physiotherapy treatment, otherwise Ross wanted him to use his crutches. He could have gone along the corridor to the day-room easily, but he insisted he was not going to do jigsaws, or cut stamps from envelopes.

'Because I've lost half a leg, it doesn't mean I've lost any brains I had as well,' he said scornfully to Karen.

'Mr Cameron,' Karen reminded him, 'you know that the occupational therapist told you that the act of leaning forward in your chair to cut out the stamps will improve your balance. It isn't just cutting out stamps, you know that very well.'

'Maybe I do,' the surgeon admitted grudgingly. He scowled at her. 'But I'm still not going along there.'

Later that day, when Ross was in, Adam said again that he was bored out of his mind.

'Yes, I hear you're not too keen on jigsaws or stamps,' Ross replied.

Adam glared at Karen.

'And you needn't look at Nurse Taylor like that, Adam,' Ross added equably. 'It's part of her job to tell me anything that might be helpful.'

'I didn't know that being an informer was part of nursing training now,' snapped Adam.

'Come on, Adam!' There was barely concealed impatience in Ross's voice, and Karen could see that he too was feeling the strain. 'You know darned well you always like a nurse who's specialling to keep you in touch with how a patient is feeling, emotionally as well as physically. Nurse Taylor's only doing her job.'

He walked over to the window and stood for a long time looking out. Then he swung round.

'How would you like to go home for the weekend?' he asked abruptly.

'Home?' Adam said cautiously. 'You mean to Lochford?'

Ross nodded.

For a moment, the tight bitterness left the older man's face. Then he turned his head.

'You know it would be too much for Mother. She couldn't cope, it wouldn't be fair to her,' he said, his voice low.

'No, I know it would be too much for her,' Ross agreed. He turned to Karen. 'Would you be able to come to my mother's house too, Nurse Taylor? Just for the weekend—maybe going on Friday afternoon, and back on Sunday afternoon? Could you manage that?'

Karen thought about this.

'I think I could,' she said, after a moment.

'What about William?' asked Ross.

'Ah, the boyfriend,' Adam Cameron said. 'Very important.'

Ross smiled.

'William is Ka—Nurse Taylor's dog,' he explained. 'I would look after him myself, but I hope to come for at least part of the weekend.'

'I could ask a friend,' Karen said.

'A strong and able friend, I hope,' Ross commented. 'Look, see what you can do, and let me know tomorrow—Mum went home yesterday, but she'd need a day or two to get ready.'

Karen had thought of asking Moira, but unfortunately the Irish girl had arranged to go away for the weekend. A little hesitantly, then, she asked Patience Mbatha.

Patience's dark eyes lit up.

'I'd love to,' she said, and Karen could see she meant it. 'To get out of the hostel for even two nights—that would be marvellous! And William and I got on well when I came round for tea.'

'He's awfully strong,' Karen warned her. The black girl was slim but sturdy, but anyone unaccustomed to William's exuberance could have a hard time.

'I have a friend who could help me to take him out,' said Patience, a little shyly. 'He's a medical student.'

The very thought of getting out of hospital for the weekend made the world of difference to Adam, Karen found. He didn't become a model patient—that would have been too much to hope for—but he was undoubtedly more appreciative of anything that was done for him, and less impatient.

She was dressing his wound on Friday morning when he said, taking her by surprise, 'I'd rather have you dressing my wound than any of the other nurses.'

Karen looked at him. 'I'm sure everyone has the same skill,' she said cautiously.

'Oh, I don't mean that,' Adam replied. 'It would be a poor show for St Margaret's if nurses couldn't bandage properly. No—I prefer you doing it because you don't say things like, "Oh, that's lovely, it's healing beautifully". Because it's neither lovely nor beautiful to me, it's ugly, and I hate thinking of it or seeing it. So thanks for keeping quiet, Nurse Taylor. By the way—my brother started to say your name the other day. Very unprofessional. Kathleen, is it? Or Katherine?'

'It's Karen,' she said.

'Karen,' he repeated. 'This weekend, Karen, would you do me two favours? First, don't wear your uniform. And second, let me just call you Karen, and let's try to forget the whole hospital scene just for two days.'

'I'll have to check with Mr Ross, and with Sister Baynes, about the uniform,' Karen said doubtfully.

But Sister Baynes agreed cheerfully that it would be much better for Adam to get away from any hospital atmosphere.

'And I'll just tell Ross that,' she said. 'He'll not mind.'

At lunchtime Karen hurried home to change into jeans and to pick up the small suitcase she had packed, and to explain to William that he would be all right with Patience. William looked mournfully at the suit-case, as if he understood what it meant.

'See you on Sunday,' Karen told him.

And when she had locked the door, leaving the key behind the stone she had told Patience about, in spite of feeling sorry for William she couldn't help her heart lifting at the thought of the weekend in the small fishing village where Adam and Ross Cameron had grown up.

And, she had to admit, the prospect of Ross's being there.

He came to see Adam settled in the ambulance, with his wheelchair packed in, and Karen sitting beside him.

'It only takes half an hour from here,' he told Karen. He looked at his brother. 'I'm hoping to be down some time tomorrow, Adam, unless anything unexpected turns up.'

And, for once, Adam had no sarcastic come-back about Ross's presence being necessary in the surgical team he himself had headed.

It was difficult to see out of the ambulance windows, but Karen managed to see that very soon they were out of the city, and heading for the magnificent Forth Bridge. Once across it, the driver turned towards the coast.

Lochford itself was just a small fishing village, and the house the Camerons lived in was just outside the village, high on the cliffs.

Karen got out of the ambulance and looked at the grey sea far below the sheer drop of the cliffs.

'What a marvellous place,' she said, delighted, as the driver and his assistant lifted the wheelchair out, with Adam in it. 'I can smell the sea!'

'And hear it,' Adam told her. 'Tonight you'll hear the waves crashing against the cliffs, and maybe you'll wish you were back in Edinburgh, with only the soothing sound of the traffic!'

Karen shook her head.

'I'll settle for the sea,' she said with certainty. 'Oh, here's your mother.'

Mrs Cameron came hurrying towards them, a stout old golden Labrador at her heels.

'You made good time,' she said, and bent to kiss Adam. Then she turned to Karen. 'My dear, we're so grateful to you for coming, and I'm not to call you Nurse, it will be Karen. Oh, and this is Tess—she's a sedate old lady now. Ross tells me you have a dog.'

'I do,' Karen replied. 'And he's not at all sedate, I'm afraid. Tess could teach him a thing or two about manners, I'm sure.'

It was ridiculous, she told herself, to feel so pleased because Ross had talked to his mother about her. But the warm glow of pleasure enveloped her, as she pushed Adam's wheelchair into the old stone house.

'You're in here, Adam, and I've put a bed for Karen in the study next door,' Mrs Cameron said.

Karen, admiring the bright little sitting-room, with a bed near the window, turned to Adam, in time to see his face tighten.

His mother had seen it too.

'I couldn't put you in your own room, dear, with the stairs,' she said quietly.

Adam smiled, but Karen could see how much of an effort it was.

'Of course you couldn't, Mother,' he agreed. 'I just hadn't thought, that's all. No, this is fine—I've always been very fond of this room. Look at the view, Karen, right over the cliffs.'

'We'll walk along the path tomorrow morning,' his mother suggested. 'That's as long as it isn't raining.'

The next morning they set off right after breakfast, for the sky was grey and threatening, and the rain not far away. Karen didn't mind, for somehow the sea, stormy and wind-tossed, looked the way she had always thought the sea around Scotland should look.

Adam had been restless through the night, and she had kept the door between their rooms open. But in spite of that she thought that already he looked better, as the wind whipped some colour into his cheeks.

'Are you warm enough, Adam?' his mother asked. 'Could you not do with another jersey?'

Adam shook his head.

'For all my life,' he said to Karen, 'my mother has been asking me if I don't need a jersey!'

'My mother's the same,' Karen told him, smiling. 'I think all mothers are.'

This is the best thing Ross could have done for him, arranging this weekend, she thought, as she pushed the wheelchair along the cliff path.

But, a little later, she wasn't so sure.

They came to a wooden seat, and Mrs Cameron suggested that perhaps they should turn and head for home. The old dog, at the word home, turned around immediately.

Karen, turning the wheelchair, looked down at Adam. His face was set, and his eyes as grey and as cold as the sea far below them.

'We used to climb down to the beach from here when we were boys,' he said, and his voice was low. 'We weren't supposed to, and we always got into trouble, because it was dangerous, but we kept on doing it.'

He turned to his mother.

'Do you remember, Mother?' he said to her.

It was a moment before Mrs Cameron answered. 'Yes, I remember, laddie,' she said, not quite steadily.

And her eyes met Karen's, in shared distress and concern.

CHAPTER EIGHT

KAREN thought, afterwards, that Adam Cameron reached his lowest point at that moment.

He sat there in his wheelchair, looking at the cliffs he had climbed as a boy, knowing and being forced to accept that there were so many things he would never again be able to do.

Karen, looking down at him, saw his knuckles tighten on the arms of his wheelchair, and she had the sudden irrational conviction that if it had been possible right then Adam would have taken himself and his wheelchair over the cliff.

'Mr Cameron, I think we should go back,' she said, not quite steadily.

He looked up, his grey eyes meeting hers, and she saw that he knew she had understood what he was thinking.

'It's all right, Karen, the mechanics of it are beyond me,' he said bleakly.

His mother had turned and begun to walk back along the path—to hide her tears, Karen was sure—and she hadn't heard or seen. Karen was grateful for that, for she thought that Mrs Cameron was showing signs of the stress she had been under since Adam's accident.

The rising wind made any conversation impossible, as they headed back to the house, the old dog ahead now, obviously thinking of the warm fire waiting for them. The cliff path was fairly level, but even so Karen was breathless by the time they reached the house.

'Right through to the fire,' Mrs Cameron said firmly, 'and I'll bring coffee through. And don't let Tess keep the heat from the rest of us, Adam.'

Her brisk, matter-of-fact tone was the right thing, Karen thought, glancing at Adam as unobtrusively as she could. The bleak grey of that moment on the cliffs had left his face, and once again the wind had given him some colour.

He made no reference to what she had seen, and what he had said, and Karen was pretty sure he never would. She would have to tell Ross, she knew that. Both as Adam's doctor and as his brother, he had the right to know.

'Coffee for you, Karen, or would you rather have tea?' asked Mrs Cameron, carrying a tray to the coffee table beside the fire.

'Coffee, thanks,' Karen replied.

Busy pouring from the tall coffee-pot, Mrs Cameron paused.

'That sounds like Ross,' she said, her face lighting up. 'Look, Tess knows too.'

The old dog, lying at the fire, was wagging her tail, but she made no attempt to get up, even when the door opened and Ross came in.

'Sorry, Mum, I'm later than I thought I'd be,' he said, kissing his mother's cheek.

He didn't, Karen thought, make any reference to why he was late, and she had noticed that he seldom referred to anything he had done in the operating theatre.

'Mud on the wheels,' he said, looking down at Adam's wheelchair. 'So you've been brave enough to go out? Just as well, because it's started to rain now.'

He smiled at Karen.

'How do you like Lochford, Karen?' he asked her.

'Very much, what I've seen of it,' Karen told him.

'She's seen nothing at all,' Adam broke in. 'I tell you what, Ross, after lunch I'll have a rest—I'm not used to all this fresh air—and Mother will put her feet up, and keep an eye on me, and you can take Karen down to see the harbour.'

Karen, ready to protest that she was here to look after him, found his eyes on her face, with something in them that she had never seen there before. He was asking her to understand, she realised, asking her to let him have some time alone, here in the house he had grown up in.

'If it isn't raining too much, I'd love to see the harbour,' she said, and some of the tension left Adam's face.

'Oh, we don't let a wee drop of rain keep us in,' Ross said easily. 'You've surely been in Scotland long enough never to move without your raincoat?'

He took the coffee his mother had poured for him and sat down at the fire, patting the old dog, whose tail was still thumping on the hearthrug.

'Soup and steamed pudding for lunch,' Mrs Cameron told them. 'And we'll have it in the kitchen, for it's nice and warm there. I hope you don't mind, Karen?'

'I'm delighted,' Karen told her, meaning it. 'We have a big kitchen at home, and we nearly always have family meals there. Can I help you, Mrs Cameron?' And then, looking at Ross, she said quickly, 'If that's all right, Ross?'

But before Ross could reply, Adam broke in. 'For heaven's sake, my dear girl,' he said impatiently, 'you don't have to be afraid to leave me for a few minutes! I can yell for you if I need to, and, anyway, have I not expert medical help right on the spot, with the brilliant young Mr Ross Cameron here?'

For a moment Ross's eyes met Karen's, questioning, but there was no chance for her to explain Adam's sudden outburst.

'I don't think you're going to need attention from either Karen or myself right now, Adam,' Ross returned equably.

Karen picked up the tray and followed Mrs Cameron through to the kitchen.

The older woman turned to her, making no attempt to hide her distress.

'They were such good friends when they were boys,' she said, her voice low. 'And even when they were growing up—and Adam, of course, always ahead of Ross—they were still close. I don't know when all this—rivalry, I suppose it is—began.'

'It can't have been easy,' Karen said carefully, 'both of them being surgeons, both of them on the same team. It would be surprising if there wasn't some rivalry between them.'

The older woman handed her a pile of woven table mats, and Karen set them at the big pine table.

'Of course, it's got even worse since they met that girl,' Mrs Cameron went on.

'She is—very pretty,' Karen said, after a moment.

'Oh, aye, she's bonny enough,' the older woman agreed. 'But she's young, and she seems to me to have very little sense. It's gone to her head a bit, the two of them vying for her attention.'

She put a plate with brown bread on it down on the table.

'I wonder, sometimes,' she said, 'whether either one

of them would have gone on being interested in her, if the other one had not been waiting his chance.'

Karen found her hands grow still on the butter dish she was holding. She thought of the Hospital Ball, and the anger on Ross's face when Adam had claimed Shona.

And then she remembered Ross's voice, when he said he would have gone on fighting for Shona if it hadn't been for Adam's accident.

'I think they're both—very much attracted to her, Mrs Cameron,' she said quietly. She could not, she knew, tell Adam's mother what he had said about being unable to live with Shona's pity. And she could not, either, tell her what Shona had said.

'Well, they can't both have her,' Mrs Cameron said practically. 'Come on, lass, let's have these boys through for some soup.'

'These boys' had obviously been disagreeing about something, Karen realised when she went into the room. Ross was standing at the fireplace, his face like thunder. Adam, in his wheelchair, looked sullen and mutinous.

'You can take me through to the kitchen, Karen,' Adam said brusquely.

'Wait a minute, Karen,' said Ross, just as brusquely. 'Adam, you're not using your crutches as much as you should.'

'I'm not ready for them,' Adam returned. 'You're pushing me too much, Ross. I don't think these crutches are the right size for me; they hurt my arms and my shoulders.'

'You're not using them properly—you should be putting more pressure on your hands. The more you use them, the better you'll get at the technique.'

Adam scowled back at him.

'Mum said on the phone that you were disappointed not to be in your own room,' Ross said unexpectedly.

Adam, taken aback, forgot to scowl.

'If you were to become more adept at using your crutches,' Ross went on evenly, 'you could cope with the stairs next time.'

'I'll think about it,' Adam said grudgingly, after a moment. 'Let's go for lunch.'

Karen looked at Ross, and after a moment he shrugged, giving in. But as she pushed the wheelchair through to the kitchen she thought he had made the point, and it did seem to have got through to Adam.

Mrs Cameron's home-made soup was delicious, and so was the steamed pudding, with golden syrup dripping down over it.

'I think that's the nicest meal I've had since I came to Scotland,' Karen said with satisfaction. She looked around at the comfortable and obviously lived-in kitchen. 'And the nicest surroundings—in a funny way, though, it's made me realise just how much I miss my family.'

Mrs Cameron leaned across the table and patted her hand.

'My dear, I take that as a great compliment.'

Ross looked at her.

'Do you get homesick, Karen?' he asked.

'Sometimes I do,' Karen said truthfully. 'Not as much now as I did at first. But this is something I've always wanted to do, and my mother and father have always encouraged us to be independent—so has my grandmother.'

She hadn't meant to go into any details about her family, but Mrs Cameron was so interested that Karen found herself telling them about her home near the beautiful gardens of Kirstenbosch, with the university and the huge sprawling hospital a few miles away, on the slopes of Table Mountain. About her father, who was an architect, and her mother, small and plump and loving. About her brothers, Jack, two years older, and Martin, three years younger, Jack in the bank, and Martin a nature conservation officer in one of the game parks.

And about her grandmother, almost eighty, small and bright and independent.

'And she still has her Scottish accent,' she told Mrs Cameron. 'She's only been back twice in all these years, but she was so excited about my coming—I write and tell her all about Edinburgh, about the hospital, and she loves it.'

'And about your difficult patients?' asked Adam.

She didn't mind the challenge in his voice, because she could see that much of the tension had left his face while she was talking, and at least for this short time he had been able to think of something other than his own problems.

'Yes, I tell her about all my patients,' she returned. 'Especially about the big bad Mr Cameron!'

'What does she say?' Adam asked, and there was something very close to a reluctant smile on his face.

'She says she'd soon have you sorted out,' Karen told him, with complete truth.

'You don't do too badly yourself,' he returned. 'You can tell your grandmother I said that.'

He looked out of the window.

'It's stopped raining, and I'm tired,' he said. 'Ross, take Karen down to see the harbour, and don't hurry back—I really would like to have a rest, and Mother is here.'

Karen got him settled in bed, and she saw that he really was tired. But in spite of her concern about him, and most of all about his reaction to being here, she did feel that he looked better for the fresh air and for the change.

She said as much to Ross, when she joined him in his car.

'I thought so too,' Ross agreed. He looked at her, and his dark eyes were serious. 'Karen, we have to talk about Adam, but not now. All right?'

'All right,' she agreed, a little unsteadily.

He started the car and drove back down the cliff road, towards the little fishing village. Down small steep cobbled streets, to the harbour, where there were houses with their front doors opening right on to the street, fishing nets stretched out for mending, and a strong smell of fish.

'Lovely!' Karen exclaimed as she got out of the car, and she wrinkled her nose in delight. 'Oh, Ross, look at the seagulls, and listen to them!'

Above them, hundreds of seagulls dipped and wheeled, their harsh cries echoing around the small harbour, and up into the grey clouds.

Ross smiled at her pleasure.

'By the way,' he said, 'did my mother ask you if you were warm enough?'

'Yes, she did,' Karen replied.

There was laughter in his eyes now.

'Then you're accepted,' he told her. 'That's a sure sign that she likes you.'

'I like her, very much,' Karen said, meaning it. She hesitated, because he had said he didn't want to talk about Adam yet. 'But Ross, she's been under so much strain with this. She manages to be cheerful and positive most of the time, but it can't be easy for her.'

'It isn't,' Ross agreed.

He looked down at her.

'Let's go and walk on the beach; it's too noisy to talk here, with these darned birds.'

They got back into the car, and he drove up from the harbour and back along in the direction they had come, but close to the sea. The beach was deserted, and the sand was firm, but quite damp, with the waves swirling up cold and grey, and topped with foam.

'You can only walk here when the tide's out,' Ross told her. 'We have about an hour before it turns. Karen, you don't have gloves, your hands must be freezing.' He took her right hand in his left and put it, inside his own hand, into the pocket of his anorak. 'Now put your other hand in your pocket,' he told her. 'We'll change when this hand is warmer.'

They walked along the beach, and there was something so disturbingly intimate about his hand holding hers, inside his pocket, that Karen could feel her heart thudding unevenly. This is ridiculous, she told herself firmly, the way you react to being near this man. Ridiculous!

But that didn't make her heart beat any more steadily.

They had been walking for some time, not saying anything, and it was a comfortable silence, Karen felt, with no pressure to break it. But when they came to a point where a narrow path wound up the cliffs from the beach, Ross stopped.

'We used to climb down from the top of the cliffs, down that path,' he said, looking up the soaring dizzy heights of the cliffs. 'Dangerous, but we looked on it as some sort of challenge.'

'I know,' Karen replied. 'Adam told me, when we were on the cliff path.'

She told him what Adam had said, and how he had looked. And then, carefully, she told him about that moment when she had seen in Adam's eyes that if he could have taken himself and his wheelchair over the cliff he would have done it.

When she had finished, she shivered, less from the biting cold of the wind from the sea than from the memory of that moment.

'It's freezing here,' Ross said abruptly. She saw that all the colour had left his face, but she had had to tell him. 'There's a cave round here—we can at least shelter from the wind.'

It wasn't a big cave, but it did, as he had said, give them some shelter. There was not a great deal of light, other than right at the entrance but even when they moved inside she knew that he was looking down at her.

'Do you think he meant it?' he asked her.

'Oh, yes,' Karen said with certainty. 'Right at that moment, he meant it. But——' She hesitated. 'But I do think it was just at that moment, when he hit rock bottom. Maybe it's like with an alcoholic; maybe he had to reach that lowest point, before he could begin to go upwards. In some ways, Ross, I don't think he had completely accepted what's happened to him, until then. Coming home was the start, and not being in his own room, and then seeing the cliffs, and remembering—it was very hard.'

Some of the colour had returned to Ross's face.

'You're very perceptive, Karen,' he said quietly. 'I

think you're probably right, I think he did have to reach that lowest point.' He was silent for a while. 'Look, will you keep me in touch with what he's feeling? In all honesty, I don't think Adam is the suicidal type, but you can never be sure. I was going to say that he probably doesn't need to be specialled for much longer, but let's stick with it at least for a few days.'

He walked to the mouth of the cave.

'We'd better walk back pretty soon,' he said. 'The tide will be coming in.'

He came back towards her, though, and took both her hands in his.

'Poor Karen,' he said, and the gentleness of his voice completely unnerved her. 'You do have a tough time with us, don't you?'

He kissed her gently.

She thought, afterwards, that that was all he had meant to do. But somehow the kiss got out of hand; his lips were hard and demanding on hers, and his arms held her close to him. And everything in her body responded to his with a wild surge she had never known in anyone else's arms.

Ross drew back, slowly, reluctantly.

'I'm not going to say I'm sorry,' he said, not quite steadily, 'because I'm not. But you do have a very strange effect on me, Karen. I suppose it must be chemistry or something, but I've never felt like this before.'

Neither have I, Karen thought, but she didn't say it. She wasn't sure if she could have said anything, right at that moment.

But one thing she was certain of. If Ross hadn't drawn back, if he hadn't released her, she wouldn't have been able to, she would have reached a point of no return. And she wasn't ready for that, because of Shona Macdonald, because of wondering whether, for Ross Cameron, she herself was just second best.

And if I am, she asked herself, as soberly as she could, is that enough?

'We'd better go,' Ross said. 'The tide is turning.'

They walked back along the deserted beach, and he kept her hand in his, inside his pocket.

And Karen, recovering, and, with her own natural optimism returning, couldn't help the thought, Perhaps for Ross it's second best, but it's still pretty good, whatever we have going for us!

CHAPTER NINE

ADAM was asleep when they got back to the house, and it was more than half an hour before he woke up.

'But I don't think he's been asleep all the time,' his mother said, as they sat at the fire drinking tea and waiting for him to wake. 'I looked in from time to time, and his eyes were closed, but I'm pretty sure he wasn't asleep.' She smiled, but her dark brown eyes—Ross's eyes, Karen found herself thinking so often—were concerned. 'I took it he didn't feel too sociable, so I pretended I was taken in, and left him.'

'I think he needed some time just on his own, Mrs Cameron,' Karen told her. 'We don't realise, sometimes, in hospitals, how little privacy patients have, especially one like Mr Cameron, who's had me or someone else with him constantly. He looks the better for both the time alone, and the sleep, I must say.'

Asleep, much of the taut strain on Adam's face had gone. It was a sounder sleep, Karen was sure, than any drug-assisted sleep he had had in hospital, and she was sure, too, that it would do him much more good.

Suddenly, loudly, the small handbell rang, startling the three sitting at the fire.

When Karen reached the other room, Adam was sitting on the side of the bed.

'I said I'd ring when I needed you, did I not?' he said. 'Well, I need you to help me into my chair.'

For a moment Karen thought of suggesting that he should come through on his crutches, but she thought that perhaps in some ways he was right, and they were pushing him too hard.

'Nice walk?' he asked her.

'Very nice,' she replied, her voice as casual as his. 'We went down to the harbour, and then we walked along the beach.'

In the evening, after they had had Mrs Cameron's steak and kidney pie, with homegrown Brussels sprouts, and potatoes from the garden, Ross, a little hesitantly, asked Adam if he would enjoy a game of Monopoly.

'You don't have to entertain me, Ross,' Adam told him. 'There's probably something reasonable on TV.'

'Yes, there probably is,' Ross agreed, and Karen saw that he was making a very real effort not to allow himself to be annoyed by Adam's reaction. 'But you can watch TV in the hospital, and you can't play Monopoly there. Besides, I thought Karen might enjoy a game.'

'Well, I don't mind, if you'd like to play, Karen—we owe you something, after all, for dragging you away from what would no doubt have been a much more exciting weekend,' Adam said ungraciously.

'I didn't have anything exciting planned, Mr Cameron,' Karen said with truth.

'Adam, when we're here,' he reminded her.

'Other than taking William for walks,' Karen went on. 'And I'm having a lovely weekend. But yes, I haven't played Monopoly for years, I'd love to—Adam.

The game soon became noisy and fun, with bids to buy property, houses and hotels, and with Mrs Cameron showing a surprising flair and an even more surprising ruthlessness, ending up owning Mayfair and

Park Lane, loading them with hotels, and charging the other three rent with great enjoyment.

'You never used to win, Mother,' said Adam, at the end.

'No, when you were small I always felt I should let one or other of you win,' his mother said serenely. 'But now that you're both grown men, I don't have to let you win. And I like winning.'

Adam and Ross both laughed, and for a moment Karen's eyes met Mrs Cameron's, and she knew they were both thinking the same—surely there was a deep and a basic bond between the brothers, a bond that could surmount the problems between them.

Karen slept well that night, and any time she did wake, and look in on Adam, she found him sleeping soundly too, either unconscious of the sound of the sea crashing against the cliffs, or undisturbed by it.

Although there was heavy rain through the night, by morning it had stopped, and the clouds were less heavy and threatening. After breakfast, Adam said he would like to be taken along the cliff path again. Ross pushed the wheelchair this time, his hands sure and strong—as they had been when he operated on his brother, Karen found herself thinking. Mrs Cameron stayed at home, saying that one good cliffside walk in a weekend was enough for her.

'Tess is getting old, isn't she, Ross?' commented Adam, as the golden Labrador walked sedately beside his wheelchair.

'She's thirteen,' Ross reminded him. He bent and patted the old dog. 'You're an old lady, aren't you, Tess?' He smiled at Karen. 'William would enjoy this, wouldn't he, Karen?'

'He certainly would,' Karen agreed. 'He doesn't

know what real freedom is, with only the Gardens to run in.'

'William is surely an unusual name for a dog,' Adam commented.

'He's called after Karen's uncle William,' said Ross, smiling.

Adam turned in his chair and looked up. 'I gather you and William know each other?' he asked drily.

'We've met,' Ross replied. 'And once met, William is never forgotten!'

Adam's grey eyes turned thoughtfully to Karen, and to her annoyance she found her cheeks growing warm. Quickly she began on the story of thinking that William was a Labrador, and gradually discovering that he wasn't.

'I look forward to meeting William some time,' Adam said, and he smiled.

But a little further on, when they reached the top of the cliff path, Karen saw that his smile had gone.

'Stop here, please, Ross,' he said abruptly.

Ross stopped, but he didn't take his hands off the wheelchair.

For a long time, Adam sat staring out at the grey, storm-tossed sea where it met the darker grey of the clouds. Neither Ross nor Karen said anything, both of them seeing that he needed to be undisturbed.

'Let's go home now,' he said at last.

Just before they reached the house, he turned to his brother.

'Ross, I hate the thought of going back in that darned ambulance,' he said abruptly. 'Could you not fit this contraption in the back of your car instead?'

'Yes, I suppose I could,' Ross replied, after a moment. 'I could put the back flat, and your chair collapses, doesn't it? Yes, sure, we can manage, Adam—I'll ring and tell them we don't need the ambulance.'

His car was an estate car, and fitting the wheelchair in wasn't difficult. Adam himself sat in the front seat, and Karen in the back.

'I'd much rather see you like this than in the ambulance,' Mrs Cameron said, when they were leaving.

Adam raised his eyebrows.

'Almost like a normal person, Mother?' he asked.

'Which is what you are, Adam, and don't you forget it,' his mother told him firmly.

She kissed him, and she kissed Ross, and then, without any pause or hesitation, she kissed Karen as well, her cheek soft against Karen's.

'I'll be in to visit Adam next week, and I'll see you then, my dear,' she said, her voice warm.

The drive back to Edinburgh, over the Forth Bridge, seemed even shorter in Ross's car than it had in the ambulance. In no time, it seemed to Karen, they were driving through the big hospital gates. The weekend was over, and she couldn't help having regrets about that.

It was already after seven, and the night nurse was in Adam's room when Ross and Karen took him up to it.

'Do you want me to help you, Nurse Harris?' asked Karen.

'Of course she doesn't,' Adam answered for his nurse, irritably. 'The girl is quite capable of getting me into bed, surely.'

Nurse Harris shook her head.

'I see we haven't come back with our temper improved,' she said sweetly.

'No, we haven't,' Adam returned.

And Karen made a mental note to tell Nurse Harris that if there was one thing Adam Cameron disliked intensely, it was to be grouped with his nurse in a royal plural.

Karen's small suitcase was still in Ross's car, and when they went downstairs she began to lift it out.

'I'll take you home, Karen,' Ross said.

'You don't have to,' she told him.

'I know,' he agreed, and smiled. 'But I want to.'

He stopped his car at the steps leading down to Karen's flat. Quickly—too quickly, she knew—she got out of the car. Ross got out too, and lifted out her suitcase. At the same time, they both saw the brightly lit windows, and heard the music from her flat.

'I suppose Patience is still here,' said Karen.

'Keeping William company, I suppose,' Ross agreed.

Karen hesitated, then asked him if he was coming in.

Ross shook his head.

'No, thanks, I'd better go back to the hospital. I want to check my theatre list for tomorrow.'

He looked down at her for a long time. And then, very gently, he touched her lips with one finger.

'Goodnight, Karen,' he said softly. 'And thanks for everything.'

And just what did he mean by that? Karen wondered, as she knocked, then pushed her front door open.

William greeted her ecstatically. She had never been away from him for this long, and she gathered that he had thought he might never see her again, and that he wanted her to know just how delighted he was to be proved wrong.

'William, for heaven's sake, I know you're pleased, but you don't have to try to knock me over!' she protested, laughing.

Patience and her medical student boyfriend were laughing too, when Karen finally managed to take her coat off and sit down, for William immediately sat on her feet, as if to make quite sure she wouldn't be able to go away from him.

'How has he been?' Karen asked, a little anxiously.

Patience and Simon looked at each other.

'He's quite a dog,' Simon said evasively.

'What did he do?' Karen queried. And when Patience hesitated, 'Go on, you'd better tell me the worst.'

'Oh, it isn't that bad,' Patience assured her. 'He just chased the ginger cat next door, and he knocked over the flowerpot with geraniums in it. Simon mended it, though, and I told the lady William was very sorry.' She looked at William with surprising affection. 'And that was a lie, I know, because you loved every minute of it, didn't you?' she asked him fondly.

William wagged his tail, but a little uneasily, for the word cat had reminded him of his sins, Karen could see.

'You're a very bad dog,' she told him severely. 'Poor old Ginger!'

Patience and Simon left soon after that, Patience assuring Karen that she'd be glad to babysit William any time.

And back to ordinary work tomorrow, Karen told herself, as she set out her uniform, pinning on her epaulettes and the badge from Groote Schuur to show that she had done her training there.

In some ways, it felt as if she had been away from

the hospital for longer than just a weekend, but very soon the familiarity of the hospital itself, and the routine, claimed her and enveloped her, and she knew she would have to work hard to hold on to her memories of the weekend in the house on the cliff.

But there was no doubt that there was a change in Adam.

Without any urging from her, he went along to the day-room on his crutches, soon after breakfast was over. To be sure, he came back complaining that 'They' had tried again to get him to cut stamps from envelopes, and he was darned if he was going to. But at least he had had some practice on his crutches.

And later, when Karen took him for physiotherapy—the physiotherapy department was a long way away, and on a different floor, and he did need his wheelchair for that— she could see that he was actually working at the exercises he had to do, not just suffering them.

She had just got back with him when Sister Newton looked in.

'Hello, Mr Cameron,' she said cheerfully. 'Do you think you could spare Nurse Taylor for five minutes?' She turned to Karen. 'Young Jenny Robertson is being discharged, and she specially wants to say goodbye to you. I'll stay with Mr Cameron while you go—I told Sister Baynes I would.'

Karen hurried along the corridor to Women's Surgical, remembering the morning Jenny had been brought in to them, remembering the anxious days when they had all wondered if she would make it. Now she was sitting on the side of her bed, dressed, and with a bright scarf tied around her head.

'But look, Nurse,' she said, when Karen commented

on it. 'My hair's growing already!' She sighed. 'It'll take ages before it's long again, I suppose.'

For a moment, Karen's eyes met Jenny's mother's, and she knew that they were both thinking, soberly, that Jenny was lucky to be alive, and the loss of her long fair hair wasn't really so important. Then Mrs Robertson gave a little shrug. She's young, she doesn't realise, she seemed to be saying.

'Anyway,' Jenny said brightly, 'Bob likes girls with short hair.'

'I hope Bob also has learned to like girls who wear crash helmets,' Karen said crisply.

'Oh, yes, Nurse Taylor,' Jenny said earnestly. 'He'd never think of letting me on the bike without one now.'

Karen said goodbye to her, and to her mother, and promised that if she was ever in Aberdeen she would visit them.

To her surprise, she could hear laughter from Adam's room, as she reached it. Adam himself didn't look at all put out, but Sister Newton looked a little pink.

'We were just remembering student days,' she said quickly. 'A long time ago, of course.'

Karen went to the door with her.

'You've cheered Mr Cameron up a lot, Sister Newton,' she said. 'I wish you'd look in more often.'

'I'll do that,' the older woman promised. 'We've been pretty busy, but we're quieter now.' She looked back at Adam. 'See you soon, Adam.'

Karen went back inside.

'She's a nice girl, Jan Newton,' Adam remarked.

'You've been friends for a long time,' I gather,' said Karen.

'Yes, we have,' Adam replied. He looked at her.

'It's a strange thing, isn't it, friendship between a man and a woman? You can be friends, or you can be lovers; it doesn't often work that you get both together.'

'Surely, if it does happen, that's the best of all?' Karen asked.

He turned away.

'I'm sure it is,' he said, his voice low.

He would be thinking of Shona Macdonald, Karen thought, and she wondered if he had any regrets about sending her away.

Somehow, because thoughts of Adam and of Shona were in her mind, she was less surprised than she might have been to have a phone call that night from Shona.

'Karen,' Shona said hesitantly, 'you did say that if I needed to talk to you again—oh, Karen, I've been doing so much thinking, and my mind's going round, and—will you come and see me, Karen? Tomorrow?'

With a little reluctance—it wasn't too easy to feel like going out, after a full day at the hospital—Karen agreed, and Shona gave her her address.

'Thank you,' Shona said gratefully. 'I—I would have come to you, but I don't want to come over to the hospital, not yet, not until I've come to some decision.'

Maybe I don't know her well enough to say this, Karen thought, but I've got to.

She took a deep breath.

'As long as it is your decision, Shona,' she said. 'I'm only too willing to come and see you, to listen to you— but you're the only one who can make any decision.'

There was a silence.

'I know that,' Shona said at last, and her voice was low.

The next night Karen hurried home, changed, took

William out, gave him his supper, did herself a piece
of chicken in her tiny microwave oven, and went off to
visit Shona.

She took the bus which went from outside the
hospital along to Princes Street, and got off just
opposite the National Gallery. Shona's instructions
were easy to follow, and she headed for George Street,
then Queen Street, and the gardens behind it. A small
street off Northumberland Street, Shona had said, and
Karen found it easily, and climbed the stairs right to
the top.

Shona opened the door. She was wearing a pink,
paint-spattered smock, and her long fair hair was tied
back from her face.

'Thank you for coming, Karen,' she said, and smiled
uncertainly.

She's shy, Karen realised, with some surprise. She's
beautiful and she's talented, but she's very shy. Somehow, the realisation made it easier for her to be here.

'I'll make some coffee,' Shona said.

Karen looked around. Shona's flat was really a
spacious attic, with a huge skylight at one end, and she
obviously used that part as a studio, for there was an
easel, some paintings stacked against a wall, and some
more on a stand.

'I'm getting ready for an exhibition,' she explained.
She looked around at the big, untidy room. 'I'm
thinking it's time I was putting things in order.'

Karen stood up.

'Do you mind if I look?' she asked.

'No, I don't mind,' Shona said.

Afterwards, Karen wondered what it was she had
expected from Shona Macdonald's paintings. Perhaps
some pretty watercolours, some Edinburgh scenes,

maybe some portraits. What she saw was, she knew, beyond her understanding—strong, clear colours, clean lines, and elongated bodies, and, although she admitted that she knew very little about art, she could recognise that there was talent and impact here.

'Stand back here, and you'll see that one properly,' Shona told her, and there was a confidence and an assurance in her voice, as she explained what she had been trying to do, that made her a different person.

And that assurance was still there when she carried the tray with the mugs of coffee on it to the big shabby couch at the other end of the room.

Karen joined her, and took a mug from her.

'I've been thinking about what you said,' Shona said then, and her blue eyes were steady. 'And you're right, of course; the only person who can make any decision is myself.'

She leaned forward.

'I'm not giving up that easily, Karen,' she said quietly. 'I owe it to Adam, and I owe it to myself, to be very sure of how I really feel about him. And tomorrow I'll come and see him, and tell him that.'

It was the right decision, Karen knew that.

But she couldn't help wondering if Shona felt that she owed it to Ross as well to give herself the chance to be certain of how she really felt about Adam Cameron.

CHAPTER TEN

SHONA came to the hospital the next afternoon.

Karen, finishing Adam's bandage, saw his face all at once become still. She looked up, and saw Shona in the doorway. Her long fair hair was loose, she wore jeans and a thick jersey, and she looked, Karen thought, like a child—a beautiful child. But her chin was resolute, and her blue eyes were steady.

'I told you——' Adam began.

But Shona broke in.

'I know what you told me, Adam,' she said. 'But you're not the only one who's allowed to make decisions.'

Karen moved away from the bed.

'You have the bell, Mr Cameron,' she told him. 'I'll be next door if you need me.'

'Don't go, Nurse Taylor,' Adam said brusquely.

'Ring if you need me,' said Karen, and went out. She couldn't, she knew, go far away, but she was not going to sit in on something as private and as personal as this was going to be.

Just to keep things right, she walked along to the duty-room and told Sister Baynes that Mr Cameron had a visitor, and she was going to the small ward next door.

'Quite right, Nurse Taylor,' Sister Baynes agreed. 'I can tell you, I'll be very glad when Dr Ross says you can stop specialling Mr Adam.' She smiled. 'Of course,

Sister Newton and I will have to put in our claims for who gets you!'

Karen had wondered about that, knowing that now both Men's Surgical and Women's Surgical were short-staffed. She knew very well that it was only because Adam Cameron was who he was that she had been allowed to special him as long as this.

There were only two patients in the small ward next door to Adam's room, and when afternoon tea arrived she was able to help the overworked nurses in the main ward, by helping the two men, one recovering from an appendectomy, the other from a fractured femur, and neither able to sit up and have their tea without some assistance.

She had just finished, when Shona Macdonald came in.

'Karen? Oh, sorry, Nurse Taylor. I'm going now— Adam asked me to let you know.'

Before she could say anything more, and before Karen could ask her, the staff nurse from the main ward came in.

'Thanks a lot, Nurse Taylor,' she said gratefully. 'The trolley's coming back for the empties, and I've only just reached here.'

'I'll go,' Shona said breathlessly. 'I'll be back tomorrow.'

So Adam had agreed, Karen thought as she went back to him.

He was out of bed, and sitting in the chair beside the window. Shona must have helped him.

He turned when she went in.

'I was not prepared to be at a further disadvantage by staying in bed,' he told her aggressively.

'That's fine with me,' Karen replied. 'Both Mr

Wilson and your brother want you to move around as much as possible.'

She tidied the bed, hoping he would stay out of it for a while, perhaps even go along to the day-room. But already she knew very well that if she suggested that he was quite likely to refuse.

'I suppose you're wondering what Shona was doing, coming back, after what I said to her,' Adam said suddenly. And, without giving her a chance to reply, 'She says she's not going to be sent out of my life like that, she says she has the right to remain my friend, to come and see me, and to take it from there.'

He was silent, but Karen's heart lifted, because he was smiling. Just a faint smile, but it softened the ruggedness of his features so much that he looked quite different.

'She's quite a girl, isn't she?' Adam said, with reluctant admiration. 'Stubborn as hell, when she makes her mind up. Well, we'll see how long it lasts— I don't see hospital visiting as being in Shona's line.'

Karen looked at him.

'You're not going to be in hospital for the rest of your life, Mr Cameron,' she reminded him levelly. And then, after a moment's hesitation, 'Not as a patient, anyway.'

For a moment she thought she had gone too far, for Adam's lips tightened. But he said nothing.

The next afternoon Shona came again. She sat with Adam for half an hour, sometimes talking, sometimes sitting quietly. Once Karen, who was in the room next door, heard them laughing. And when Shona left there was a tide of warm colour in her cheeks, and her head was high, as she told Adam that she'd be back the next day.

She hadn't been gone long when Mrs Cameron appeared.

When she had greeted Karen, and kissed Adam, she said, very casually, that she thought she had seen Shona Macdonald leaving, as she parked her car.

'You probably did, Mother,' Adam replied evenly. 'She's just been visiting me.'

'About time too,' his mother said. 'I must say, I thought she would have been here long before this, considering the two of you were seeing such a lot of each other before——'

She stopped.

'Before I had an accident and lost half a leg?' Adam asked. And, before his mother could reply, he went on, 'The reason she hasn't been here, Mother, is that I told her I didn't want her to come.'

'You didn't want her to come?' his mother repeated.

Adam shook his head impatiently.

'I didn't want her pity,' he said. 'And I still don't. But—well, Shona says I have no right to assume it *is* just pity. She says we owe it to ourselves to give ourselves the chance to find out.' He shrugged. 'And she tells me she'll be coming every day, and I'm not to stop her.'

His mother was silent for a long time.

'Good for her,' she said at last, a little faintly.

Sardonically, Adam smiled.

'Changes the picture of her you had in your mind, doesn't it, Mother? I suppose you thought she'd be only too glad to get out of any involvement with a cripple.'

'Oh, Adam,' his mother said unsteadily. 'I wish you wouldn't speak of yourself like that.'

Adam raised his eyebrows.

'Why not?' he returned. 'You always taught us, when we were boys, to face facts. And I have to accept that, you know I do.'

But somehow, in spite of the bleakness of his voice, Karen couldn't help feeling that his whole approach had become more positive. Whether the change had started with the weekend visit to his home, or with Shona's decision, she didn't know, but she was only too grateful.

Adam began using his crutches more, even though he was still scathing about the occupational therapy provided in the day-room. He stopped grumbling about being taken for daily physiotherapy, and grumbling when Karen reminded him that it was time to do the exercises he was supposed to do on his own.

And a few days later, when Ross was in, Adam said to him, abruptly, 'What's happening about the insurance on my car? I gather it was a write-off.'

For a moment Ross's eyes met Karen's. 'It was,' he agreed cautiously. 'I've been dealing with the insurance, Adam; it didn't seem necessary to bother you with it. There's no question of liability on your part, of course, so it will only be a matter of time for the claim to go through.'

'I suppose it will take a while to order one of these special cars?' said Adam, looking beyond his brother, and out of the window.

'I can find out about that,' Ross replied, his voice still careful.

Adam swung round.

'I certainly don't intend being dependent on other people to take me around,' he said aggressively.

'No, of course not,' Ross agreed. He hesitated for a moment, then said, 'Frank Wilson was telling me he's heard of a surgeon in Lincoln. He didn't have to lose a leg, but his leg was pretty badly hurt, and he can't stand for too long. He's had a special seat made, so that he can move in close to the operating table; he can work for fairly long periods, and all with his leg supported.'

'Oh, no,' Adam said, his voice treacherously soft. 'Oh, no. Ross—I'm not prepared to play at being a surgeon, with carefully chosen and undemanding operations to do, and people saying, Isn't he marvellous, and him missing half a leg? No, thank you! I'd rather be a GP.'

Ross said nothing, and Karen's heart ached for the hurt and the rejection on his face.

'You could do worse than that, Mr Cameron,' she said, before she could stop herself. 'You would have a great deal of understanding to bring to being a GP now.'

But Adam had had enough.

'You'd better let me see these insurance forms,' he said coolly. 'I'm quite capable of dealing with my own business affairs, thanks.'

Don't mind so much, Karen wanted to say to Ross. Don't let him hurt you. But she could not, for that would have been much too unprofessional.

She was pretty sure that Adam had said nothing to Ross about sending Shona away, and telling her he did not want her pity. Ross must surely have wondered if Shona had carefully timed her visits so that she wouldn't see him. And of course, being Ross, being determined not to take advantage of the whole situation, he would not have gone near her since that day when he had brought her to see Adam, and Adam had accused him of not wasting any time.

And because of all that, Karen could see the shock, the immediate raising of defences on Ross's face, when he came into Adam's room the next day and found Shona there.

She herself had met him as he strode along the corridor.

'Ah, Nurse Taylor, deserting my brother, are you?' he asked cheerfully, without pausing.

'He has a visitor with him, so I thought——' Karen began.

'Good, that should cheer him up,' Ross said, going into Adam's room.

That was when he saw Shona. She was sitting on the windowsill, and Adam was in the chair beside her, and she was telling him about the painting she had to finish for her exhibition.

'And I can't get that light right,' she said, frowning. 'You see, Adam——'

She stopped, then, and a slow tide of colour flooded her face.

'Ross,' she said awkwardly. 'I—haven't seen you for ages.'

'No, your visits and mine haven't coincided,' Ross agreed. 'I'll come back later, Adam—I had a break in my theatre list, but I'll be back up here to see a couple of fellows just before I go off. See you then.'

He looked at Shona. 'I hope your exhibition goes well, Shona,' he said politely. 'Where is it to be?'

'In that little gallery not far from Holyroodhouse,' Shona told him, still a little awkward.

When she thought about it afterwards, Karen was never sure whether Ross did what he did as some reaction to Shona and Adam, or whether he did it because he wanted to.

He turned to her.

'We could have a look at Shona's exhibition, couldn't we?' he suggested.

As if, Karen thought sadly, they were in the habit of doing that sort of thing together.

But she wanted to help him; she would have done anything, she realised afterwards, to support him.

'I'd like that,' she replied, and smiled at him. 'You know, I've never been to Holyroodhouse.'

Ross raised his eyebrows.

'Never been to Holyroodhouse?' he repeated. 'I bet your grandmother's shocked at that!'

'I've been to the Castle,' Karen told him. 'I did that in my first week here, and I went up the Scott Monument, and I took photos of the Floral Clock, but somehow I didn't get around to Holyroodhouse.'

'That settles it,' said Ross. 'Holyroodhouse, and Shona's exhibition. We'll fix it.'

Karen found Adam's grey eyes resting thoughtfully on her face.

She lifted her chin and looked right back at him.

I don't really mind what Ross's reasons were, she thought, with some surprise. If he remembers, if we do have a day together, I'll enjoy it.

The next day, when she went to the door with Ross after he had inspected and been satisfied with the healing of Adam's wound, he said to her,

'Can I have a word with you, Nurse Taylor?'

'Certainly, Mr Cameron,' Karen replied, just as formally.

In the corridor, he smiled down at her. 'When are you off?' he asked, taking her by surprise.

'Saturday,' she told him. 'Only from lunchtime, though.'

'That should give us long enough,' he said. 'I have a short theatre list, so I'll be clear by lunchtime too. I don't think the art exhibition will have started, but how about Holyroodhouse?'

'I'd like that,' Karen replied, and wondered how her voice could sound so sedate, when her heart was thudding unevenly against her ribs.

On Saturday, Ross came to pick her up, although Karen said she could have saved time by meeting him closer to the hospital.

'It's just an excuse to say hi to William,' Ross told her.

And William, bounding up the steps the minute Karen opened the door, obviously thought that was the sole purpose of Ross's visit, to see him. He found his well-chewed tennis ball and brought it to Ross, laying it down hopefully at the young surgeon's feet.

'I'm sorry, William,' Ross told him, with real regret. 'Maybe when we get back we'll have time.'

He looked at Karen appreciatively, and she was glad she had decided to wear her brightly patterned woollen skirt and her suede boots, instead of trousers.

'You look nice, Karen,' he said. 'But will you be warm enough? Holyroodhouse is pretty draughty.'

'I have my thick jacket,' she told him. And then, unable to keep back a smile, she said, 'Ross, you sound just like your mother!'

He smiled too. 'I suppose I do,' he agreed.

He was wearing dark brown trousers and a thick cream Aran jersey. He looked—different, somehow, Karen found herself thinking, and she couldn't put her finger on just what the difference was.

Until he turned to her, as he parked the car.

'There's something I want to say, Karen. It isn't easy, and I'm not particularly proud of myself, but I have to say it. The other day, in Adam's room—it threw me, seeing Shona unexpectedly, seeing Adam and her, the way they were. I suggested doing this for some sort of childish paying them back—I'm not too sure what I was thinking.'

She had thought that was why, but somehow, hearing him say it, admit it, hurt her.

Then he looked down at her and smiled, a slow, warm smile.

'But do you know something?' he said. 'By the next day, when I asked you when you were off, there was only one reason for doing it. Because I wanted to. I want to show you Holyroodhouse, I want to hear what you think about Mary Stuart and Bothwell, I want to see you when we go into the room where Rizzio was murdered. I—maybe I shouldn't have said any of this, but it's important, somehow, to have things clear between you and me.'

Karen's throat was tight.

'It's important to me too, Ross,' she said, after a moment. 'And I'm glad you told me.'

They left the car and went into the forecourt of the Palace.

'We're lucky,' Ross said with satisfaction. 'It's too cold and too like rain for many other visitors.'

He pointed out the carved Gothic fountain in the centre, and told her that Prince Albert had had it put there.

'I suppose it's Mary Stuart's apartments you want to see most?' he asked her.

Karen nodded, all at once breathless at the realisation that she was here, where the tragic young Queen had lived and where she had had so much unhappiness.

'The staircase—my gran told me about it,' she murmured, as they came to the narrow staircase which had been used by both Darnley and Bothwell.

She wasn't sure when it was that Ross took her hand in his, but by the time they reached the room with the brass plate marking the spot where Rizzio was murdered her hand was firmly in his.

Karen stood very still, thinking of the shocked young woman, heavily pregnant, realising how she had been betrayed, and realising the danger to herself and to her unborn child.

'I suppose,' Ross said, a little later, as they walked round the portrait gallery, 'you'll be telling me that your sympathies are with Mary and Bothwell?'

Karen, interested in the tragic love story, had read enough to know that there were many different thoughts on the true relationship between the young Queen and the brash, arrogant nobleman.

'I know it probably isn't as romantic a story as I'd like it to be,' she said, after a moment. 'I suppose after he kidnapped her she didn't have much choice but to marry him. But what was it she's supposed to have said? That she'd follow him to the ends of the earth in her petticoat?'

Ross's brown eyes were very dark, as he looked down at her.

'You would be like that too, would you not, Karen? You would be as loyal and as loving, if you gave a man your heart?'

It was a moment before she could answer.

'Yes, I think I would,' she said unevenly.

CHAPTER ELEVEN

KAREN thought, afterwards, that somehow that moment when Ross looked down at her, unsmiling, was more intimate and more disturbing than if he had kissed her.

For he didn't kiss her.

He didn't even touch her. For a lifetime, it seemed to her, he stood there close to her, his dark eyes holding hers.

And then, deliberately drawing them both into a lighter mood, he smiled, the slow, warm smile she was beginning to know so well.

'Let's go and take William out,' he said.

William was overjoyed to see them both, bounding from Karen to Ross, bringing Ross his ball, running back to where his lead was hanging and looked at it hopefully.

'Walk nicely, William,' Ross told him sternly, and snapped the lead in the approved fashion.

And Willaim walked, head and tail high, as if he were in a show ring.

'When I do that, he just turns and grins at me,' said Karen, walking beside Ross and the dog into the Gardens.

'I wondered if I'd just imagined that grin,' Ross said. 'The last time, when he brought the ball and dropped it, he just flashed his teeth at me.

'Oh, yes, he does smile,' Karen agreed. 'He's done it since he was a puppy.'

'The Labrador we had before Tess used to smile,' Ross said.

They had reached the open part in the middle of the park, and let William off the lead. The dog ran round and round in wide circles, and Ross shook his head.

'I don't think I've ever met a dog quite as enthusiastic, somehow, as William is,' he said.

He looked down at Karen and smiled.

'You look chilly, Karen,' he remarked. 'Let's have a good brisk walk, right round the park.'

He took her hand in his, easily, casually, and began to walk, whistling to Willaim. Karen had to walk quickly to keep up with Ross's long strides, and soon she could feel her cheeks glowing.

They were both breathless by the time they got back to the flat. Somehow there didn't seem to be any question as to whether or not Ross was coming in, and soon Karen found herself taking two steaks from her small deep-freeze, and trying to look as if she always kept that sort of thing handy.

'Baked potatoes in your microwave,' said Ross, with satisfaction. 'And grilled tomatoes, and peas. Good, you've got everything we need.'

'You're quite domesticated,' Karen said, laughing, as she began to scrub two large potatoes.

'I find cooking very relaxing,' he told her. 'You won't know, being with Adam all the time, but we've had quite a theatre list the last couple of days, so I'm only too glad to get into a kitchen.'

'Not much of a kitchen,' Karen said ruefully, thinking of his mother's spacious kitchen in the house on the cliffs.

'Nice and friendly,' he returned, as they bumped into each other.

It was a very successful meal, and Karen was glad she was able to produce a piece of Brie and some biscuits, with coffee.

'I have enjoyed the day,' Ross said with satisfaction, draining his coffee-cup. 'And I think William has enjoyed his share of it.'

William was stretched out in front of the fire, fast asleep.

'So have I,' Karen agreed. And then, because she realised all at once just how close they were, on the couch in front of the fire, she asked quickly if he wanted any more coffee.

'Yes, please,' he said, and she got up to boil the kettle.

A few moments later, with his cup of coffee in her hand, she stopped.

Ross was fast asleep, his head fallen back on the big cushion at one end of the couch. He looked much younger, much more vulnerable, she thought. Just for a moment, she could almost see the boy he had been, the boy who had followed so faithfully in his older brother's footsteps.

She put the cup of coffee down, and then, very gently, eased Ross into a more comfortable position, but he was so soundly asleep that she was even able to put his feet up on the couch. She went back over to the small sink and washed the dishes, stacking them in the drip tray, but doing it all very quietly.

When she had finished, she saw that the fire had gone down. Putting on more coal would disturb Ross, so she took a blanket from one of the other chairs and put it over him. Just as she was tucking it in around him, he opened his eyes.

Sleepily he smiled, and put his arms around her, drawing her down beside him.

It was a big couch, but she was very close to him. Too close, she knew, disturbed by his body against hers. Then he kissed her, his lips warm but demanding, and she knew that even this close wasn't close enough.

Suddenly, shrilly, his bleeper sounded.

'Damn!' he said forcibly.

His thick fair hair was rumpled, and his eyes were still sleepy, but the spell was broken.

Silently Karen pointed to her phone, near the door.

While he spoke, she pushed her hair back from her face, and sat up on the couch. And waited for her uneven heartbeat to steady itself.

'I have to go to the hospital,' he said, coming back to her. 'Emergency appendectomy, and Frank Wilson is tied up with a perforated ulcer in the other theatre.'

Karen took his coat from the hanger near the door.

When he had put it on, he looked down at her.

'Maybe it's just as well,' he said quietly. 'I'm—pretty confused about the way I feel about you. If we hadn't been interrupted, I might have been even more confused.'

And I would have been completely lost, Karen thought, when he had gone. But deep inside, she knew she had been lost from the moment she looked down at Ross's sleeping face.

'Have a nice afternoon off, Nurse Taylor?' Adam asked conversationally, when she went on duty the next morning.

'Very nice, thank you,' Karen replied, checking his chart.

'Do anything interesting?' Adam asked, his voice casual.

In spite of herself, Karen could feel her cheeks growing warm.

'Yes, I went to Holyroodhouse,' she said, not looking up from the chart she was studying.

'Alone?' he asked.

But Karen had seen something on his chart that disturbed her.

'I'm just going to take your temperature and your pulse-rate, Mr Cameron,' she said, knowing all too well that her casual tone would not deceive him for a moment.

His eyebrows shot up.

'Why?' he asked her. 'Nurse Winter did them before she went off duty.'

'I know that,' Karen agreed, and put the thermometer in his mouth, and held his wrist. 'I just want to re-check.'

He glared at her, but with the thermometer he was helpless.

Methodically, she entered both temperature and pulse-rate. Both slightly up. Not much, but with a post-operative patient there was always the danger of deep vein thrombosis, especially because, owing to his amputation, there could be no venous drainage from the lower extremity on his right leg.

'I have no stiffness, no pain, and no oedema,' Adam said levelly. 'Check for inflammation, Nurse Taylor.'

There was no inflammation in his upper leg, and Karen knew that that was not a good sign. Without inflammation, there was a far greater danger of the thrombus embolising, leading to pulmonary embolism.

'No inflammation,' she told him. 'I'd like your brother to have a look at you, Mr Cameron.'

Adam didn't argue. His face was drawn and suddenly grey, for he knew all too well how dangerous this could be.

Karen dialled the theatre number, and asked for a message to be given to Mr Ross Cameron as soon as possible. She hesitated, then added that it was extremely urgent.

Tem minutes later Ross appeared, his white coat obviously hastily put on when he came out of Theatre.

'I'm sorry to have to call you, Mr Cameron,' Karen said. 'But I thought it was necessary.'

She told him what she had observed, making no comment, knowing it was unnecessary.

Swiftly he examined his brother, his hands strong and sure. Adam said nothing until he had finished.

'What are you going to do, Ross?' he asked.

'Ultrasonic Doppler flowmeter,' Ross said.

'Accurate, rapid and non-invasive,' Adam agreed, but Karen saw how much of an effort it was for him to show no emotion. 'And then?'

'If we find a clot, we'll remove it surgically,' said Ross. 'I'm not prepared to risk a pulmonary embolism, Adam.'

'Neither am I,' Adam agreed levelly. 'Neither am I, Ross.'

Ross turned to Karen.

'Good work, Nurse Taylor,' he said. 'I'll go and get this set up; I'll have someone from Theatre here as soon as possible.'

He was at the door when Adam called him back.

'Ross!' he said urgently. And when Ross strode back

to the bed, 'Get them moving fast, Ross. I don't want to die.'

For a moment, Ross's hand covered his brother's.

'I won't let you, Adam,' he said.

When he had gone, Adam turned to Karen.

'Sorry about the heavy emotion, Nurse,' he said, and tried to smile. 'Funny, a couple of weeks ago, I really didn't give a damn. Now—I'm not giving up.'

Within an hour, he had been taken down to the theatre, the Doppler test having confirmed that there was a clot, and he was in surgery.

There was nothing Karen could do but wait. She had asked Sister Baynes whether she should let Mrs Cameron know, but Sister Baynes thought it was better to wait until the operation was over.

And since his mother was not being informed yet, it seemed wrong to let Shona Macdonald know. But Karen, knowing what time she usually came, was hoping to catch her before she went into the room. Unfortunately the young artist came earlier, and Karen, coming back from lunch, saw, from one end of the long polished corridor, Shona pushing open the door of Adam's room.

'Hi,' Shona said cheerfully when Karen reached her, a little breathless from hurrying. 'Is Adam in the day-room? I'll go along and meet him.'

'No, he isn't,' Karen replied.

There must have been something in her voice, or in her face, she realised, for all the colour drained from Shona's face.

'There's something wrong,' she said, and it wasn't a question.

Quietly, factually, Karen told her what was being done, and why no time could be wasted.

'And this clot—if it reached Adam's lungs, it could be dangerous?' Shona asked.

'Yes, it could,' Karen replied. She hoped the girl didn't realise just how dangerous it could be. 'Sit down, Shona, I'll make you a cup of tea.'

An hour later, she pointed out to the girl, gently, that even when the operation to remove the blood clot was over Adam would be kept in Intensive Care for at least twenty-four hours.

'Wouldn't you rather go home?' she asked. 'I'll phone you as soon as there's any news.'

Shona shook her head.

'I'd rather stay here,' she said stubbornly. 'If I'm not in the way?'

It was another hour before Sister Baynes came in with a message from Theatre. The operation had been successful, the clot had been removed, and Mr Cameron was in Intensive Care.

'I thought you might like to phone his mother, Nurse Taylor,' Sister suggested. 'You know her better than I do.'

She looked at the fair-haired girl sitting huddled in the chair beside the empty bed.

'Go home, my dear,' she said kindly. 'Mr Cameron is in the best hands for immediate post-operative care. Give me a ring tomorrow, and I'll tell you when he's coming back to us.'

Obediently Shona stood up. At the door, she turned to Karen.

'Will you let me know, Karen, if—if anything goes wrong?' she said, not quite steadily, and Karen promised that she would.

But by the time Karen went off duty—having spent the rest of the day on the overworked and understaffed

Men's Surgical Ward—the news was that Adam was already making a good recovery, and would be brought back to the surgical floor the next day.

'Big drama with your special, I believe,' said Moira Sullivan, sitting down beside Karen in the canteen just after ten the next morning. 'Are you getting him back today?'

'Probably this afternoon,' Karen told her. 'But in case it's earlier, I'm on early tea and early lunch. How are things on your ward?'

'Busy,' Moira told her briefly. 'But Sister Newton keeps things moving—sure and she's a bit bossy at times, but maybe that's how you have to be, when you're a sister.'

From the far side of the room, Patience Mbatha waved, and came over to join them.

'How long does this weather go on?' she asked, looking out the window at the steadily pouring rain.

'It's only November,' Moira said, laughing. 'We still have months of this, Patience.'

The black girl shook her head. 'When I think of the sunshine I left behind,' she said. 'And you, Karen, summer just beginning in Cape Town—how can you bear it?'

'By not thinking about it,' Karen told her. 'Anyway, Patience, there are compensations about Edinburgh— I thought you'd found that out for yourself.'

'Maybe,' Patience agreed. 'Remember, Karen, if you ever need a babysitter for William I'll be delighted.'

'I'll remember,' Karen replied. She looked up at the big clock. 'Time I was back on the ward. See you later.'

It was early afternoon when Adam was brought back from Intensive Care. Karen, determined not to show the anxiety she had been feeling, knew how unsuccessful she had been when Adam, his voice surprisingly strong, said to her,

'You look as if you're surprised to see me back again, Nurse Taylor. Surely you didn't think one small clot was going to succeed where one big lorry failed?'

Ross had come up to the surgical floor with his brother. For a moment his eyes met Karen's, and he smiled.

'Your patient is in surprisingly good spirits, Nurse Taylor,' he told her, and she could hear the lift in his own voice. He looked down at his brother. 'I suppose you think you're pretty clever, giving us all a fright like that.'

'Got to do something to liven things up around here,' said Adam, but his eyes were heavy, and a few minutes later he was asleep.

'He's come through it remarkably well,' Ross said soberly. He hesitated. 'This isn't very professional, but I can't help feeling that something in his attitude has changed. He isn't bitter, as he was before.'

Adam slept for most of the rest of that day. Karen disturbed him as little as possible, doing the hourly temps that were necessary, checking his pulse-rate, examining his dressing. She kept the light in the room dim, using a small torch.

Just before she went off duty, when she was doing her final pulse-rate check, Adam opened his eyes and looked at her.

'You remind me of the story about Florence Nightingale,' he said. 'She was doing her usual Lady with the Lamp business, when one of the Crimean soldiers said to her, "Flo, for Pete's sake put out that ruddy lamp, and let us all get some sleep!"'

Completely taken aback, Karen burst out laughing, the next minute looking anxiously at the door, in case anyone had overheard such unprofessional behaviour.

'I'm sorry if my lamp disturbed you, Mr Cameron,' she said laughter still in her voice, not only at his story, but at his cheerfulness.

And that cheerfulness continued to surprise her—to be sure, there were times when the old impatient and arrogant Adam Cameron showed in his face over the next few days. His mother came to see him, and Shona came, and both said to Karen, privately, that, worried as they had been, the anxiety had almost been worth while, because of the change in Adam's attitude.

It was Ross who commented on it to his brother.

'The whole thing pulled me up short, Ross,' Adam admitted, after a moment. 'It made me realise two things. First, that I didn't want to die. And second, that I'm darned if I'm going to let this——' he touched his right leg '—get me down. How soon can I get out of this place, Ross?'

Karen could see that Ross was taken aback by the abrupt question.

'I'll have to think about that,' he said cautiously. 'I'll see what Frank Wilson says.'

'The sooner I can lead a normal life, the better,' Adam said. 'I'm fed up with being in this room, and being treated as a patient.'

And the next day, when Karen came back from having lunch, he said to her,

'You'll be glad to be back to being Staff Nurse Taylor, instead of Mr Cameron's special, I'm sure— just as I'll be glad to see the last of this room!'

'It's been very interesting,' Karen said cautiously. And then, with sudden intuition, she went on, 'But you know, Mr Cameron, you've had all this time of being here, of people looking after you—although you're looking forward to getting out, don't you feel a little insecure, at the thought of going it alone?'

He looked at her.

'That's extremely perceptive of you, Nurse,' he said. 'And yes, I do feel more than a little insecure. I keep wondering how the heck I'll manage!'

Wondering if she was exceeding her duties, Karen told Ross about this conversation, when she met him in the corridor later.

'I'm not surprised at him feeling like that,' he said slowly. 'What I am surprised at is his admitting it. You've been very good for him, Nurse Taylor.'

The next day she came back from her tea-break to find Adam out of bed, in the armchair, his crutches beside him, and Ross sitting on the windowsill.

'We've just had an expedition,' Adam told her, 'and we've had a talk.' He looked at his younger brother. 'Over to you, Ross.'

Ross's dark eyes held Karen's.

'I think,' he said slowly, 'that it's time my brother got out of hospital and into a more normal setting. I suggested a week in a convalescent home, but he isn't interested.'

'No way,' said Adam, with certainty.

Ross shrugged.

'My mother isn't really able to cope with him on her own.' He hesitated. 'What we wondered, Adam and I, is this—would you be prepared to take a week's leave of absence and come to Lochford? I think a week with you there would give Adam the confidence he needs— you could take him for the daily physiotherapy he'll still need, go with him as he moves around the house, and in general keep an eye on him.'

'If you agree, we'll be able to square it with Sister Baynes, and with Matron,' Adam put in. 'What about it, Nurse Taylor?' He hesitated, then said awkwardly, 'I would really appreciate it. It would make quite a difference to me.'

Karen didn't know what to say. She walked across to the window.

In so many ways, she felt it would be unwise to have any further involvement with the Cameron family. Going to their mother's home, to look after Adam, would inevitably mean seeing more of Ross. And she didn't know if that was a good idea.

But first and foremost, she reminded herself, she was a nurse, and Adam Cameron was her patient.

She turned round, her mind made up.

'I'll come,' she said quietly.

CHAPTER TWELVE

Ross insisted on Adam's staying in hospital for another week, and Karen was glad of that time, to make arrangements to go away.

Patience was delighted to come and stay in Karen's flat, and Karen could see that she meant it when she said she would enjoy looking after William.

Sister Baynes suggested that Karen should ask for two weeks of the leave due to her.

'Mr Cameron might not need you that long,' she said. 'But a week seems to me very short for him to make all the adjustment he'll have to. Because after you leave someone will still have to bring him for physiotherapy, I can't help feeling it will all be a bit much for his mother.'

She hesitated.

'It's quite a thing, Nurse Taylor, to give up your holiday time, you know. Unfortunately, even Adam Cameron being who he is, there's no way we can justify sending you back with him.'

'I don't mind that,' Karen said truthfully. 'I did think I'd like to spend a week walking in Normandy, but by the time the weather is good enough for that I'll have some more leave due.'

Adam himself, a little brusquely, said he appreciated what she was doing, and so did Ross.

'We couldn't have discharged him, if you'd refused,' he told her. 'And I wouldn't have blamed you at all, giving up your leave, coming away from Edinburgh, and leaving William.'

But it was Moira Sullivan who expressed the concern Karen herself had.

'Is this wise, Karen, until you know how Ross really feels about this girl? Aren't you just looking for trouble?'

'I don't know,' Karen admitted. 'Maybe I am. Shona Macdonald comes every day to see Adam; sometimes I think things are going to work out for them, but sometimes I think they won't. And if that happens then I don't know if she'll turn to Ross.' She smiled at her friend. 'But after all, Adam is my patient, and I wouldn't like to let him down at this stage.'

Ross took Adam and Karen to Lochford in his estate car, with the wheelchair folded up in the back, and Adam's crutches beside it.

'I went over to your flat and packed some things for you,' he told his brother. 'I hope I haven't left out anything you'd want, but I can always go back.'

Adam shrugged.

'I shouldn't think I'm likely to be leading a very active social life,' he said evenly. 'So I won't need much. Thanks, anyway, Ross.'

As Ross drove along the cliff road towards the house, Karen could see how tense Adam was. He sat up straighter, and his knuckles were clenched. This was more than just a weekend visit, with the security of the hospital at the end of it; this was the beginning of his changed life.

'I've put you in your own room, just as you said,' Mrs Cameron told him, when she had greeted them all—kissing Karen as easily and naturally as she kissed her sons. 'But the stairs worry me—are you sure you'll manage, Adam?'

'Yes, Mother, I'm sure,' Adam returned. And then, obviously ashamed of his brusqueness, he freed one arm from his crutch, and hugged her. 'Don't worry, Mother, I've been practising. And I can't spend the rest of my life avoiding a few stairs, you know.'

But in spite of his practising—and through that last week, Karen had taken him to the physiotherapy department twice a day, so that he could have extra practice with his crutches, on the specially constructed stairs, and under the eagle eye of Nora Hunter, the physiotherapist—Karen's heart was in her mouth as she stood at the foot of the stairs and watched him make his way up, moving his crutches to the next step, then swinging his body, awkwardly, determinedly. Once she moved instinctively to go to him, but Ross's hand closed on her arm.

'Leave him,' he said, his voice low. 'He has to be allowed to be independent.'

'I know that,' Karen replied. 'But what if he falls?'

He looked down at her, his brown eyes very dark.

'He will fall,' he told her evenly. 'But his wound is healed, and it's well protected, and maybe he has to fall, and pick himself up, and get on with his life.'

Adam had reached the top of the stairs now. Holding on to the banister, he raised one crutch and waved it to them.

'I feel like Hillary on top of Everest,' he said. 'You can all breathe again!'

Karen, turning to lift one of Adam's suitcases, saw that his mother was very white. But she tried to smile.

'Thirty-eight years ago,' she said, not quite steadily, 'I watched him taking his first steps, and I wanted to go to him and catch him, before he fell. But I knew I had to let him try, and I know I have to do the same now.'

She straightened her shoulders.

'I think we all need a cup of tea,' she said briskly. 'Ross, will you build up the fire, and see that Tess isn't lying right in the door, where Adam might fall over her?'

When they were having tea, she told Karen that she was in the small guest-room next to Adam's.

'I'm glad you're not wearing uniform,' she said approvingly. 'I think we've all had enough of hospitals.'

'She isn't wearing uniform because she's on holiday,' Adam told his mother. 'Haven't you heard that Lochford in late November is regarded as one of the most desirable holiday spots?'

Mrs Cameron turned to Karen.

'Is that right, Karen?' she asked, taken aback. 'Is this your holiday?'

'Well, there wasn't any other way to do it,' Karen explained. 'And I don't mind, really, Mrs Cameron.'

And she meant that. Sitting here, in this warm and comfortable room, with Ross on the couch beside her—and a swift and very disturbing memory of that all too short time when she had been in his arms on her own couch—she had the sudden certainty that, whatever happened, she was determined to have no regrets about this time.

'I tell you what,' said Mrs Cameron, 'when winter's over, I'll ask my cousin Helen if we can go to her cottage in Skye for a week. You'll love Skye, Karen, and I'm sure your grandmother would love to think of you going there.'

'Oh, she would,' Karen agreed. 'She spent her

honeymoon on Skye, and she says no one will believe her when she says they were there for a week, and it didn't rain!'

'I certainly don't believe her,' said Ross, smiling. 'I've never yet been on Skye when it didn't rain.'

He put his cup down.

'I'm sorry, Mum,' he said with regret. 'I have to get back—I have a couple of unexpected things on my theatre list, so it will take longer.'

'What are they?' asked Adam unexpectedly.

Ross, already standing up, looked down at his brother.

'A thyroidectomy,' he said carefully, 'and a laryngectomy.'

'Total?' Adam asked.

Ross nodded. Karen could see that he was unwilling to say anything more, because of Adam's previous reaction to any mention of the theatre team they had both been part of.

'Malignancy of both the vocal cords?' Adam asked.

Ross shook his head. 'The subglottic part of the larynx,' he said.

'Watch out for a pharyngeal fistula,' Adam told him.

Karen's heart lifted, because there was no trace of bitterness in Adam's voice, and no trace of resentment in Ross's.

'I'll do that,' he replied.

He was at the door, when Adam said, 'That fellow you mentioned in Lincoln, the one who had a special chair made—I wouldn't mind hearing a bit more about him.'

'I'll see what I can find out,' Ross promised, and went out.

Five minutes later he came back in, his anorak on,

to say goodbye. When he had kissed his mother, and said goodbye to Adam, he said casually, 'Coming out to the car with me, Karen?'

Her face warm, Karen rose.

'Don't go outside without a coat, Karen,' Mrs Cameron called.

'I won't,' Karen promised.

And, even in spite of her warm jacket, she shivered when they went outside.

'Not too nice for getting Adam out,' said Ross, 'but do it as much as you can.' He looked down at her. 'I can't say how grateful we all are to you, Karen. I really do think he's turned the corner now—not so much physically as emotionally. And without you coming with him he would have had less confidence about coming here. You'll manage my mother's car all right, for taking him to physiotherapy? It's smaller than mine, but a hatchback, so you'll get the chair in all right.'

'I'll manage,' Karen assured him.

He took both her hands in his.

'I like to think of you here,' he said.

For a moment, his lips brushed hers, then he got into the car and drove off. Karen stood watching until he turned the corner, her lips still warm from his brief kiss. Then she went back into the house.

Part of her job in this time, she knew, was to encourage Adam to be as independent as possible—but with the security of knowing that she was there.

And so, over these first few days, she forced herself to listen to the muffled curses, the sudden loud outbursts, as sometimes he dropped one of his crutches, or as he struggled to dress himself. Occasionally he would open his mouth and call for her imperiously. But unless he did she forced herself not to go to him.

One morning he did stumble as he was coming down the stairs. Karen, at the foot, saw him lose his balance, drop one crutch, then fall down the last three steps.

'Damn!' he said explosively.

And then, without another word, he took his remaining crutch, hauled himself back up the few steps to where the other one was, got himself to his feet again, and came down, successfully this time.

His visits back to the hospital for physiotherapy were down to every second day now, and Karen, knowing that Adam would be more tired than he might admit, had arranged them for mid-morning, so that he could rest in the afternoon. But when they came back from the first physiotherapy visit, and she suggested he should have some lunch, and then rest, he shook his head.

'I'm not an invalid,' he told her brusquely. 'I might sit at the fire for a bit, but no more. Anyway, I want to make a phone call.'

Expert on his crutches now, he swung his way into the hall. With the phone in his hand, he turned to his mother.

'All right if I ask Shona to come tomorrow, Mother?' he said casually.

Karen wondered if she had imagined the slight pause before Mrs Cameron replied, equally casually,

'Of course, dear. Tell her to come for lunch.'

Karen, watching Adam becoming increasingly restless and impatient as the morning drew on, saw his face clear as he looked out of the window and saw Shona arrive.

But he went back to his chair by the fire then,

looking up casually when Mrs Cameron brought her in, as if, Karen thought, amused and somehow touched, he didn't really care whether she came or not.

'Did you come through much rain, Shona?' Mrs Cameron asked politely.

'Solid,' said Shona. She smiled a little uncertainly. 'I have an uncle in Glasgow, and when it rains like that, he's always saying it's comin' doon hale watter.' She turned to Karen. 'That means, Karen, that it's coming down whole water.'

'I understood,' Karen assured her. 'Don't forget I have a Scottish background too; I'm not entirely an outsider!'

It was much too wet to go out, and after lunch Adam said he was teaching Shona to play chess. Mrs Cameron went to her room to put her feet up, and Karen said—with complete truth—that she had letters to write, and she wanted to sit at the big kitchen table to write them.

Sometimes, in the next couple of hours, she heard laughter from the sitting-room, and sometimes just voices. But she didn't go through until Mrs Cameron came down, and they made tea.

'You must go soon, Shona,' said Adam, as they were having tea. 'I don't want you driving when it's too busy, and getting dark.'

For a moment Karen saw his mother's hand grow still on her cup, at the authority in his voice when he spoke to the fair-haired girl. Almost, she thought, as if he had the right to tell Shona what to do.

And rather to her surprise, Shona didn't seem to mind. As soon as she had finished her tea, she stood up.

'Thank you very much for having me, Mrs Cameron,' she said gravely. Like a small girl at a party, Karen thought, with a surprising wave of affection. And a small girl who wasn't too sure whether or not she had been welcome.

'Thank you for coming, Shona,' Mrs Cameron returned. And then, obviously as conscious of Adam's grey eyes on her face as Karen was, she said, 'Do come back any time.'

'Thank you,' Shona replied. And then, her colour high, she said, 'I was wondering if I could come the day after tomorrow, when Adam doesn't have to be going for physiotherapy?'

'Of course, if you want to,' Mrs Cameron replied quickly. A little too quickly, Karen thought, and she saw Adam glance at his mother as if he thought the same. 'But haven't you an exhibition just now?'

'Yes, I do,' Shona replied. 'But I don't have to be there unless I want to.'

The implication was clear—that she'd rather be here, with Adam.

'She's a nice enough girl,' Mrs Cameron said to Karen, a little later, when they were peeling potatoes together. 'But she's so young, and I can't forget that she seemed to have difficulty making up her mind between the two of them.' She turned her head, but not before Karen had seen that there were tears in her eyes. 'I suppose I just don't want either of my boys to get hurt, and it seems to me that one of them is sure to. Although I do wonder if Ross——'

Her voice trailed away, and Karen, knowing that she was over-sensitive to anything and everything about Ross, tried, with no success, not to comment on this.

'What do you wonder about Ross?' she asked casually.

Mrs Cameron shrugged.

'I just think that maybe it's the old rivalry thing, between the two of them,' she said. 'Because Adam wanted Shona, so did Ross. Or he thought he did.' She smiled, and shook her head. 'I wonder if all mothers find it impossible to give up—not worrying about their bairns, but being concerned for them. Even when the bairns are grown men and women.'

'My mother is just the same,' Karen assured her. And a tide of colour flooded her cheeks as she thought of her mother's last letter, saying to her, 'Tell me more about this Ross Cameron. Sometimes you mention him; sometimes you don't. I can't help feeling he's important to you, Karen.'

'That should be enough potatoes,' Mrs Cameron said briskly. 'And enough of me worrying about things I can do nothing about! For it will make no difference to Adam what I think of this lassie. It certainly will not be bothering her.'

But two days later, when Shona came again to visit Adam, she followed Karen through to the kitchen when Karen went to make tea.

'Is Adam's mother resting?' she asked, for she had arrived later.

Karen said she was.

Shona sighed. 'I don't think she likes me very much,' she said, her voice low. 'Oh, she's always very nice, but I wish I could feel that she liked me. Especially now.'

Karen waited.

'In some ways,' Shona said slowly, 'this whole thing has been very good for us, for Adam and me. We've become friends, Karen. Before, we were in love, or we were close to it, and everything was very exciting, we were always doing things, going places.' Her blue eyes were very clear, as she said candidly, 'I must admit, I liked being seen with Adam, I liked people looking at the two of us together.'

If I don't ask it now, I never will, Karen thought.

'And Ross?' she asked carefully.

'Ross?' Shona looked surprised. 'Oh, Karen, I was never really interested in Ross, not in the same way. Right at the start, perhaps—it was quite something, you know, two good-looking brothers, and both of them wanting to date me, but it was always Adam I was interested in.'

Karen set the teapot on the tray and looked at Shona levelly.

'Then it's a pity you didn't make that clear to Ross,' she said.

Shona coloured. 'I should have,' she agreed. 'But surely he must know now?'

'I'm not too sure if he does,' Karen returned, more tartly than she had meant to. 'Just take this tray through, will you, Shona? I'll boil some more water.'

While she was boiling the kettle again, Mrs Cameron came into the kitchen.

'Karen, would you mind if I just took some tea and went back upstairs? I'm a wee bit tired,' she said apologetically.

Karen, busy at the cooker, turned round. The older woman's eyes were shadowed, and there was a grey tinge to her skin that she didn't like at all.

'You're not well, Mrs Cameron,' she said, concerned.

'I've just been doing a bit more than I should. The doctor says——' Mrs Cameron stopped.

Karen went to her and took both her hands in hers.

'Sit down here, Mrs Cameron,' she said, and led the

older woman to one of the kitchen chairs. 'And tell me just what the doctor says.'

'Only if you promise me not to tell Adam or Ross,' Mrs Cameron returned.

Karen hesitated.

'I'm not promising anything,' she said honestly. 'Not yet, anyway.'

'I've got a touch of heart trouble, but I have my pills for it, and really, Karen, I'm fine as long as I don't do too much.' She sat up straight. 'But I will not have Adam worried about this, or he'll think he shouldn't be here. I'll be more careful, after this.'

There was a sound at the door. Neither Karen nor Mrs Cameron had heard Shona come back.

'I forgot the spoons,' she said. She looked directly at Mrs Cameron. 'I couldn't help hearing, Mrs Cameron. I agree with you, it wouldn't do Adam any good to know, right now. So I'll tell you what we're going to do.' Her chin was high, and her eyes steady. 'I'll come and stay for a bit. I can cook, I can do shopping, I can clean if you need me to.'

Mrs Cameron shook her head.

'Jessie MacPherson comes up three times a week from the village,' she said, bewilderment in her voice. 'But why should you do that? You have your own life, your own career, in Edinburgh.'

The two women looked at each other, the older woman's dark brown eyes holding the younger woman's clear blue eyes.

'I think you know why, Mrs Cameron,' said Shona. 'Because Adam is important to me, and anything to do with Adam is important to me. I want to help.'

'Shona, I'm waiting for my tea!'

Adam's voice, and the sound of his wheelchair

approaching. In the doorway of the kitchen, he stopped.

'What is this?' he asked suspiciously. 'A Women's Only meeting?'

It was his mother who recovered first.

'A bit of a conference, Adam,' she said easily. 'I was just saying what nonsense it is Shona driving up and down every second day, so we've decided it would be better if she came to stay for a bit. What do you think of the idea?'

For a moment there was a blaze of joy on Adam's face that made him look years younger. Then he was more controlled, more restrained.

'I think it's a good idea,' he said casually.

But Karen, following the others through the hall, found herself wondering what Ross would think when he came next and found Shona Macdonald here.

CHAPTER THIRTEEN

ONCE Mrs Cameron had accepted that Shona was coming to stay, she obviously made up her mind to do it with a good grace.

The next day, before Shona arrived, Karen found her in the small spare room next to the kitchen, setting out pretty guest towels, arranging a small bowl of flowers.

'I could have done all this, Mrs Cameron,' Karen told her sternly.

'I'm fine, Karen, really. I've been doing things slowly,' the older woman assured her. And Karen had to admit that she did look much better now.

'Remember, now,' Mrs Cameron said, her voice low, 'there's no need to say anything to Adam or Ross.'

'Maybe not at the moment,' Karen agreed. 'But as soon as possible you must tell them. It's not fair not to. I would want to know if there was anything wrong with my mother.'

She looked around.

'This is a pretty room, Mrs Cameron.' She hesitated. 'You don't think Shona will mind being so far from the rest of us?'

The other bedrooms were upstairs, and there was another spare room, very small, but beside the other bedrooms.

'Och, that room was just a boxroom, it's awfully small,' Mrs Cameron said quickly.

'Then, colour flooding her cheeks, making her look all at once younger, she shrugged.

'All right—I didn't think it was a good idea to put Adam and her so close,' she said, a little defiantly. 'They're both in an emotional state right now. I may not be young any longer, but I haven't forgotten how young people feel.' For a moment, her brown eyes were dark with memories. 'Duncan and I met during the war,' she said quietly. 'We were often separated, we seldom knew when we would see each other again, and that makes things difficult for a young couple.'

She sat down on the chair beside the bed.

'It isn't the same for Adam and this girl,' she said. 'And I don't want you to think I'm so old-fashioned that I don't know that things have changed a great deal nowadays. But whatever decision they make, these two, I want them to make it clear-sightedly. And that's why I'm just helping them to avoid a situation that might cloud their judgement.'

You dear lady, Karen thought, and affection for Mrs Cameron swept through her. You don't want them to sleep together, but you can't quite bring yourself to say so.

Impulsively, without knowing she was going to do it, she hugged the older woman.

'With a mother like you,' she said, not quite steadily, 'I'm sure Adam has a background of wise judgement to draw on.'

Mrs Cameron returned her hug.

'Oh, my dear, I do wish——' she began, then stopped. 'Well, we'll see about that,' she said. 'Dearly as I love both my laddies, I must admit there's times when I could shake them!'

Shona arrived soon after lunchtime, with a small

suitcase and a large rucksack of sketching books, an easel, and a folding stool.

'I didn't put you upstairs, Shona, because sometimes Karen has to get up to Adam, and I didn't want you to be disturbed,' Mrs Cameron said untruthfully and unblushingly.

'Oh, that wouldn't bother me, I sleep like a log,' Shona said cheerfully. 'But this is fine, Mrs Cameron— I'm close to the kitchen, and that's handy for making breakfast.' She took out a small notebook. 'Now,' she said briskly, 'just tell me when mealtimes are, and if there's anything anyone doesn't like.'

'I didn't expect you to be so—so organised,' Mrs Cameron said, obviously taken aback. 'I'd have to think about all that.'

Shona shut the notebook.

'I'm not,' she admitted. And then, disarmingly, 'I just thought I'd make a good impression if I was organised.'

Mrs Cameron smiled, a slow warm smile that was so like Ross's smile, that Karen knew once again why she liked his mother so much. She patted Shona's hand.

'Let's just take things as they come, my dear,' she said. 'Anyway, it will have to look as if you're just helping me, not taking over, otherwise Adam will wonder what's going on.' She looked at Karen. 'What's he doing, anyway?'

'Reading books on surgery,' Karen told her. 'I think—well, maybe I just hope—that he's turning his mind to what sort of surgery he might be able to do.'

Shona was putting her clothes into the small wardrobe.

'When will he get his artificial leg?' she asked, and her long fair hair hid her face.

'That depends on the whole healing process,' Karen told her. 'It could be weeks, or it could be months.' Casually, then, she said, 'You could ask Ross, when he comes.'

'He's coming for the weekend,' said Mrs Cameron. 'He says he'll be down as early as possible on Saturday morning.'

But a little later, when she and Karen were alone, and Shona had taken Adam out for a walk along the cliff path between showers of rain, she asked Karen if she thought it would be better to let Ross know that Shona was here.

'I think it probably would,' Karen replied, her voice as casual as Mrs Cameron's had been.

'I'm not going to phone him specially to tell him, though,' Mrs Cameron said. 'I refuse to make a big deal of this. If he phones, I'll tell him; if he doesn't, he can just find out when he comes!'

Shona's coming to stay had taken a great deal of responsibility from Karen as well, for it was Shona who took Adam out in his wheelchair when he wanted to go—or when she thought he should go—and it was Shona who sat and talked to him when it was too cold and wet to go out. And when, as sometimes happened, his spirits were low.

'Stay here and talk to me,' Adam said imperiously on Thursday afternoon, when Shona rose to go and cook a chicken for their evening meal.

Laughing, Shona pulled her hand away from him and shook her head, her long fair hair falling over her face.

'You can't have everything revolving around you, Adam,' she told him. 'I want to try this new chicken recipe, and, besides, your mother has plenty to do; she can do with some help.'

She bent and kissed his cheek, unselfconsciously, not worried by the presence of either Karen or Mrs Cameron.

'You sit here, Mrs Cameron,' she said, 'and put your feet up—if Tess will allow you to, anyway—and I'll see to things in the kitchen.'

'I'll give you a hand with peeling veggies,' Karen offered, and the two girls went through to the kitchen together.

With surprising efficiency—at least, Karen realised, she found it surprising—Shona set to work on preparing the chicken, making an oatmeal stuffing.

'I'm sure that's the stuffing my gran makes,' Karen said. 'Do you put egg in it?'

Shona shook her head.

'No, it doesn't need it,' she said.

'Neither does she,' said Karen, and began to peel the potatoes. 'Shona,' she went on, after a moment, finding it somehow easier than she had thought to talk to this girl, as they worked together in the kitchen, 'it's very nice of you, coming here to help, but you do have your own life, and your own career.'

Shona's blue eyes were clear and steady.

'Yes, I do, and my career is important to me,' she said. 'I couldn't live without painting, but I don't think I could live without Adam, either.'

'Does he know how you feel?' Karen asked.

'If he doesn't, he must be blind,' Shona replied. And then, disarmingly, 'But I'm not all that noble, Karen, coming here to help. I—I want Adam's mother to like me, to accept me, and maybe this will help.' She put down the fork she had been using to mix the stuffing.

'I think she's made up her mind about the sort of person I am, and she's not prepared to see that perhaps she's not entirely right.'

She smiled.

'And besides, it gives Adam and me more time together, and we need that.' Her blue eyes were shadowed now. 'I'm thinking, Karen, that I've done some growing up since all this happened, and I'm thinking, too, that perhaps I needed to.'

Involuntarily, Karen remembered Shona dancing at the Hospital Ball, her skin golden against her white dress, her long fair hair shining. And young enough to be flattered when Adam claimed her from Ross. Dancing, if it was possible for Adam, would never again be the way it had been that night.

She finished the potatoes, and cleaned some carrots which Shona had set out.

'Have you talked, you and Adam, about his leg?' she asked.

'Not enough,' Shona replied. 'I think it's more of a problem to Adam than it is to me, but I'm not sure if he realises that.'

She finished stuffing the chicken and tied it neatly in place.

'You've noticed, I'm sure,' she said quietly, 'that he always makes some excuse to send me away when you're changing his dressing. That's one hurdle we have to get over, but I can't rush him.'

Karen, thinking of Mrs Cameron admitting that she had taken a deliberate decision to put Shona in the bedroom downstairs, had a sudden growing uncertainty that perhaps the longer this necessary closeness was put off the more difficult it would be for both Adam and Shona.

'I wouldn't be too sure about that,' she said, her voice level. 'If you and Adam are going to spend the rest of your lives together, you have to be close enough—in every way—for him not to mind.'

There was a slow, warm tide of colour in Shona's face, and Karen saw that she had understood what Karen was saying.

'I'll think about that,' she replied, not quite steadily. 'That should be enough carrots, thanks, Karen.'

Without being too obvious about it, or so Karen thought, she managed to find out, the next day, that Ross hadn't phoned, so he wouldn't know about Shona being here. She hoped that when he arrived on Saturday, either she or his mother would hear him coming, and be able to tell him she was here. Mrs Cameron seemed to feel that it wouldn't trouble Ross too much, and, although Karen wished with all her heart that that would turn out to be the case, she wasn't certain.

And she wasn't certain, either, whether she wanted to lessen the shock of his just suddenly coming face to face with Shona, here in his own home, so that he wouldn't be hurt, or so that she herself wouldn't have to see his reaction.

Never, she thought restlessly around midnight on Friday night, as she lay in bed unable to sleep, had any man had this—bothersome—effect on her before.

She closed her eyes and breathed deeply, determined to sleep. Then she sat bolt upright, for there was a sound downstairs. A door, closing softly—and footsteps. There was someone down there. Her thoughts whirled. Shona had said she slept soundly, so she wouldn't hear anything. Neither Mrs Cameron nor

Adam could be of much use. Old Tess slept in Mrs Cameron's bedroom, and she was very deaf now.

There's only me, Karen realised, her heart thudding unevenly.

Quietly she got out of bed, and slid her feet into her slippers. Then she tied her warm blue dressing-gown around her and went downstairs as silently as possible. The door to Shona's small bedroom, she could see, was closed, so, as she'd thought, Shona had heard nothing.

In the hall, Karen carefully lifted a stout stick from the hallstand. The kitchen door was closed, and it was usually left open. The intruder must have come in the back door and closed the door to the hall. But the light was on in the kitchen.

Karen gripped the stick in her right hand and threw open the door, ready to hit out with the stick.

The bright light dazzled her, and she couldn't help blinking, just for a moment.

When she opened her eyes, she saw Ross sitting at the kitchen table. Astonishment gave way to amusement as he looked at her, taking in the stout stick, the dressing-gown. And, she realised, her untidy, sleep-rumpled hair, and her clean but unadorned face.

'I suppose you thought I was a burglar,' he said, unable to keep his lips from twitching, and he got up and closed the kitchen door again. 'All I can say is I'm mighty glad I'm not! Were you really going to lay into some poor fellow with that?'

'You shouldn't creep in like that, giving everyone a fright!' Karen told him indignantly and inaccurately, since she was the only one who had heard. 'Why didn't you phone to say you were coming?'

Ross was still smiling.

'Did you know your hair is standing on end?' he

asked her, and put out one hand and smoothed it down. 'Well, I didn't phone because I only heard late that the gastric resection I was supposed to do tomorrow morning has been re-scheduled for Monday, and suddenly I was free. I thought I'd come down now, and have the whole weekend here. I was just going to have something to eat.'

There was something that was all at once very disturbing about the amusement in his dark brown eyes, about his closeness to her in the quiet kitchen in the middle of the night.

'I'll make a sandwich for you,' Karen said quickly. She took some cheese from the fridge, and some Branston pickle from the cupboard, and spread two slices of bread. When she had finished, she found that Ross had heated milk and made two mugs of cocoa.

They sat at the big pine kitchen table, close to the embers of the fire.

'I think a kitchen should have a fire,' Ross commented. 'I don't like these shining white kitchens you can't be comfortable in.'

'I like the fire too,' Karen agreed. And then, because the intimacy of the two of them here together disturbed her, she asked him about the hospital, about his theatre list, how busy things were on the surgical floor.

Obediently he answered her questions. Then he leaned across the table and took her mug and his own, and carried them across to the small couch beside the fire.

'Come and sit down, Karen,' he said.

'I don't think I should,' Karen replied.

Ross set the cocoa mugs down and reached out for her hand.

'Why not?' he asked her, and sat her down on the couch beside him.

'It's late,' Karen said quickly. 'You've had a long drive, you must be tired, and—and——'

And this is your mother's house, she thought, her heart thudding against her ribs because he had his arm around her shoulders. And I'm here in a professional position, and——

There was laughter in his voice, deep, warm sleepy laughter that completely unnerved her.

'I'm not going to seduce you,' he said. 'I just want to sit here, quietly and peacefully and pleasantly, for a little while.'

His arm was warm around her, and gradually she relaxed. He was quite right, she thought drowsily, it was indeed very pleasant.

'Maybe I want to do a little more than just sit here,' Ross murmured, and gently he turned her face towards him and kissed her. It was a slow, warm kiss, and Karen, still drowsy and relaxed, could do nothing but enjoy it thoroughly.

And then, quite suddenly, his lips left hers.

'I think perhaps you were right,' he said, not quite steadily. 'It's late, and you'd better go, Karen.'

And once again she wasn't sure whether she was disappointed or relieved. She stood up and put her mug back on the table.

'Goodnight, Ross,' she said, not quite steadily.

'Goodnight, Karen,' he replied.

As she opened the door, she remembered that she should tell him about Shona.

'Ross,' she said hesitantly.

'For heaven's sake, girl, you're undermining all my good resolutions!' he told her.

But she had to tell him.

'Shona Macdonald is staying here,' she said baldly.

He lifted his head.

'Why?' he asked, and his voice was cool and abrupt now.

'Your mother asked her to,' Karen told him, knowing that was all she could say.

Ross said nothing else, and after a moment Karen went out, and upstairs to her room. And rather to her own surprise she slept soundly for the rest of the night, waking, a little disorientated, to hear Adam calling for her.

Quickly she pulled on her dressing-gown and hurried through to his room.

Her patient was already up and dressed.

'I just wanted you to know that I managed without you,' he told her cheerfully. 'Are we too early, do you think, or will Shona be making breakfast?'

'Give me five minutes to wash and dress, and I'll go down,' Karen replied. She still preferred to be around when he went up and down the stairs, although very soon he'd have to do it on his own. 'Oh, Ross came last night, very late.'

She didn't wait for his reply, but hurried back to her own room to dress.

Shona was making scrambled egg when Karen and Adam went into the kitchen. Adam, quite expert now with his crutches, made his way across the kitchen to her and kissed her.

'To think I thought you were just decorative,' he said. 'Shona, Ross is here—apparently he arrived late last night.'

Shona turned round.

'I didn't hear a thing,' she said. 'Did you let him in, Karen?'

But before Karen could reply, Ross himself did.

'No, I let myself in,' he said, from the door. 'Karen thought I was a burglar, and she came in armed with Granddad's stick. Quite a surprise, seeing you here, Shona, and making yourself very useful, I see.'

He sat down at the big kitchen table, and Karen thought he was the only person in the room who was entirely at ease.

Shona, stirring the eggs, looked flushed and uncomfortable, Adam was guarded, and she herself could not free herself from the sudden and disturbing memory of the two of them, Ross and herself, in this same kitchen, alone, just after midnight, and Ross's lips warm on hers.

'It seemed a good idea, Shona coming,' said Adam, a little awkwardly. 'It was Mother's idea, actually—she said it seemed ridiculous Shona driving down so often. I must say I didn't realise that Shona had talents other than her artistic gifts. Yes, she is making herself useful.'

There was a note of—defiance, almost, Karen realised, in his voice.

Ross said nothing, but picked up the morning paper and glanced at the headlines.

'You don't mind, do you?' Adam asked him.

Ross put the paper down, and raised his eyebrows.

'Mind?' he said, surprise in his voice. 'Why on earth should I mind?'

And Karen, looking at him, and at Adam and Shona, couldn't help thinking, If only I could be sure you really meant that, Ross.

CHAPTER FOURTEEN

IT WAS only afterwards that Karen could admit to
herself how much she had been looking forward to the
weekend, and Ross's being there.

And how different it was from her hopes.

They did the things she had hoped they would, she
and Ross. They took the old dog for walks along the
cliffs, and they talked about how much William would
enjoy this. They went back to the old harbour and
watched the fishing boats come in, laden with their
silvery catch, and they listened to the seagulls as they
wheeled and soared above the harbour. They sat at the
fire, with the rain beating against the windows.

And yet there was something missing.

There seemed to be a distance between Ross and
her, a distance there hadn't been before. She knew
very well that it was because of Shona, but she couldn't
blame Shona herself, for it was all too obvious that all
she wanted was to be with Adam.

And perhaps that, Karen thought bleakly, was the
trouble, that Ross was at last having to accept that his
brother was Shona's choice.

On Sunday morning, when Adam and Shona were
sitting at the fire playing chess, Karen went through to
the kitchen to put the kettle on for coffee. Mrs
Cameron and Ross were there, and they looked, she
thought afterwards, a little awkward, a little embar-
rassed, when she went in. Whatever they had been
talking about was obviously not meant for anyone else

to hear, for Mrs Cameron stopped almost in mid-sentence. Karen wondered, for a moment, if Mrs Cameron had decided to tell Ross about her heart problems, but Ross didn't look like someone concerned and even anxious. No, she decided, that wasn't what they had been talking about.

'I thought I'd make coffee,' she said, feeling awkward herself.

'Good idea,' Mrs Cameron replied brightly.

Ross said nothing. But sometimes, through the rest of that day, Karen found him looking at Shona, unsmiling, his eyes very dark.

When he left, it was raining, and he had drawn his car up close to the door. He said goodbye to Adam and Shona, and his mother rose to go to the door with him. Karen, because she didn't think he wanted her to, sat still.

'Come along, Karen, let's make sure he gets on his way,' Mrs Cameron said cheerfully, linking her arm through her tall son's. Karen, her cheeks warm, rose, after a moment's hesitation, and went out with them. Because, she told herself sensibly, it was easier, and less fuss, than saying she wouldn't bother.

'Oh, Ross, I have some of these oat biscuits for you,' Mrs Cameron said, as they reached the door. 'I'll just get them from the kitchen.'

Ross looked down at Karen.

'Better keep that stick handy, in case you have any burglars,' he said, and smiled.

And, in spite of everything, her heart lifted, for this was much more like the Ross she had come to know.

Then he wasn't smiling any more.

'Karen,' he said abruptly, 'my mother thinks——'

He stopped. 'No,' he went on, almost to himself, 'this isn't really the time.'

His mother came back, then, with a small tin.

'I'm glad I remembered,' she said, 'because I made them specially for you; they were always your favourites.' She handed him the tin. 'When will we see you, Ross?'

'Probably the weekend,' Ross replied. 'I might look down, if I have a day with a short theatre list, but don't count on it.'

He kissed his mother, and then, with only a brief hesitation, his lips brushed Karen's cheek too.

When his car disappeared round the corner, and they closed the door, Karen wondered if Mrs Cameron would make any reference to whatever she and Ross had been talking about. But the older woman said nothing, and Karen reminded herself that it was nothing whatsoever to do with her. After this week she would go back to the hospital, Adam would learn to cope—obviously with Shona's help—Ross would have to accept Shona's choice, and life would go on.

She took Adam through for physiotherapy the next day, and arranged that from the following week he would go to a physiotherapist near Lochford, so that either his mother—or perhaps Shona—could take him.

'And as soon as possible,' Adam said on the way home, his jaw set, 'I'll drive myself, and be independent.' He glanced down at his leg. 'Ross had a look at the weekend, and he thinks it won't be too long till I can be fitted for my prosthesis. I told him it can't be soon enough.'

Karen glanced at him. 'You know very well these things can't be rushed,' she reminded him. 'You'll have to be patient.'

Adam shook his head.

'You must know very well by now, Karen, that whatever else I am I'm not patient!'

And then, with an all too obvious change of subject, he asked her if she had had time, while he was having physiotherapy, to see her friend on Women's Surgical.'

'She wasn't on duty,' Karen told him. 'I'll give her a ring tonight.'

She had wanted to talk to Patience, to find out how William was, and had been disappointed to find that she was off duty.

'Oh, he's fine,' Patience told her when she phoned that night. 'A little quiet, but that's all. He's eating, and he enjoys his walks. Don't you, William?'

William, a little quiet? Karen put the receiver back slowly, disturbed.

And when Ross phoned, half an hour later, and she answered, he asked immediately if everything was all right.

'Yes, everything's fine,' she assured him.

'I thought you sounded a bit worried,' he said.

'Not about anything here,' Karen told him. 'It was just—I phoned Patience, and she says William's a little quiet.'

'William quiet?' echoed Ross. 'I find that hard to believe!' And then, his voice warm even over the phone, 'Look, Karen, it would be surprising if he didn't miss you, now wouldn't it? And William being quiet probably brings him into the range of ordinary dogs! Don't worry about him, I'm sure he'll be fine.'

It was absurd, but somehow she did feel better about William.

'Did you want to speak to your mother?' she asked him.

Ross said not really, if Karen could just pass on the message that he'd be through for the afternoon on Wednesday, but would have to leave around seven.

'The day after tomorrow—how nice!' Mrs Cameron said, her face alight, when Karen told her. 'Just as well it isn't tomorrow—didn't Shona say she might take Adam for a drive?'

'If it isn't raining,' Karen replied.

The next day was one of these surprisingly mild November days that helped the coming winter to be acceptable, Karen thought. Soon after lunch, she helped Shona to load the wheelchair in the back of her car, and they set off, with a Thermos filled with coffee.

'Just so that you can stop wherever you want to,' Mrs Cameron explained, waving as they left. She turned to Karen. 'I really wondered how Adam would feel about going in anywhere for a coffee,' she said. 'I thought it would be easier if they had it with them.'

Karen hesitated.

'That's something he has to get used to, Mrs Cameron,' she said gently. 'Perhaps the longer he puts it off, the more difficult it will be.'

Mrs Cameron's brown eyes were shadowed.

'Maybe you're right, lass,' she agreed. With difficulty, she smiled. 'Anyway, if Shona thinks she can persuade him to go in anywhere, she'll do it.' She shook her head. 'I must admit I'm developing a healthy respect for the girl's judgement, where Adam is concerned.'

But when it was getting dark, and Adam and Shona hadn't returned, she was less certain about Shona's judgement.

'She doesn't know the roads, and anyway, Adam's been out long enough,' she said anxiously.

And when the phone rang she hurried to answer it.

Karen, walking through the hall, saw her face tighten.

'Oh, Adam,' she said, not quite steadily, 'are you sure that's a good idea?'

There was a short silence, as she listened.

'Yes, I know you're old enough to make your own decisions, but you can't stay away for the night and no pyjamas or toothbrush with you!'

There was another silence, then she put the telephone down and stared at it, disbelieving.

'What did he say?' asked Karen, unable to contain herself.

'He laughed!' Mrs Cameron said indignantly. 'He laughed, when I said they had no pyjamas or toothbrushes! Do you know what they're doing, Karen? They're at St Andrews, Adam says, and they're going to stay there tonight—in a hotel—and come back tomorrow morning. What do you think of that?'

I have to be honest, Karen told herself. For everyone's sake.

'Mrs Cameron,' she said carefully. 'I think that perhaps it's a very good idea. If Shona and Adam are going to spend the rest of their lives together, and it's beginning to look as if they are, then—then the sooner they get any possible difficulties out of the way, the better. You—do understand what I'm saying?'

The older woman's eyes searched her face.

'Yes, my dear, I understand,' she said at last. 'I'm just afraid that spending the night together will make them less clear-sighted about any decision.'

Karen shook her head.

'I think it's the other way round, Mrs Cameron,' she said quietly. 'I think this is something they have to do, now, before they know how they feel about any long-term decision.'

Mrs Cameron sighed.

'You may be right,' she said unexpectedly. She turned away, but not before Karen had seen that there were tears in her eyes. 'It's just—I couldn't bear Adam to be hurt any more.'

And he could be, Karen thought soberly, through the next morning, as they waited, each trying to hide her anxiety. He could be badly hurt, if—things don't work out for him and Shona.

When the car drew up she saw Mrs Cameron take a deep breath, and deliberately walk outside slowly, and she followed the older woman.

One glance at Adam's face, and at Shona's, told her all she needed to know about how things were between these two. The caution had gone, and she could see the commitment. Over the weeks she had seen friendship grow between them, a warm and caring closeness. But now there was more than that—much more.

Mrs Cameron had seen it too, and Karen was glad there were no questions, no recriminations. Just an acceptance.

'Well, Mother,' Adam said, a little awkwardly, as he got himself out of the car, leaning against it until Shona gave him his crutches.

'Well, Adam,' his mother returned. 'No need to ask if you enjoyed being at St Andrews—I can see you did. How was the weather?'

Adam and Shona looked at each other.

'Cold?' Adam said tentatively.

'And rainy,' Shona agreed.

They smiled at each other. There was no need to say any more.

Ross would see, when he came this afternoon, Karen thought. He would see, and he would know. And perhaps once he had accepted this, really accepted it, he might——

She had wondered, once, if she could live with being second choice for Ross. Now, in complete honesty, she thought she could live with that more easily than she could live without him.

After lunch Adam agreed, with some reluctance, to have a rest. Shona, her face flushed, her eyes glowing, took her sketching block and went off down to the harbour. Mrs Cameron went to rest too.

And Karen waited for Ross to come.

Restlessly, she moved around the comfortable living-room, building up the fire, boiling and re-boiling the kettle, looking at the clock. She could, she knew, walk along the cliff road to meet him, but she resisted that thought. Until three o'clock struck, and all at once she was too impatient to wait any longer. She needed fresh air and exercise, she told herself, as she zipped up her anorak and pulled on thick gloves.

There was no sign of any car on the road. She walked briskly, glad in any case to be outside. And then, when the road fell steeply towards the village and the harbour, she turned and walked back towards the house.

She was halfway there when she heard the sound of a car, but she would not allow herself to look round. It might not even be Ross, she told herself sternly.

But the car slowed down as it caught up with her, and the hooter sounded imperiously. Karen turned round as it drew up beside her.

She had one minute to see the surprising sight of William sitting on the passenger-seat beside Ross, large and regal, and looking as if Ross was his chauffeur.

Then William saw her, and with yelps of excitement launched himself out of the door Ross leaned across to open.

With his paws on her shoulders, he peered earnestly into her face, as if to reassure himself that this really was his beloved mistress.

'Down, William!' shouted Ross, and obediently William got all four paws on the ground. But only for a moment, before he launched himself at Karen again.

This time he caught her off balance and knocked her down.

Ross, laughing, took both her hands and pulled her to her feet.

'Sit, William,' he said sternly, and William sat. His pink tongue lolled out of his mouth, and his tail kept on thumping on the ground.

'Are you all right, Karen?' Ross asked.

'I think so,' Karen replied. 'It isn't the first time William has knocked me off my feet.'

Ross opened the back door of the car for William, but the dog ignored this, and got back into the front seat.

'I'll go in the back,' said Karen.

'No, you won't,' Ross told her firmly. 'This fellow has to learn that he isn't the boss. Back seat, William!'

It took ten minutes for William to realise that Ross really meant this, and then, with a canine equivalent of a shrug, he climbed over as if it had been his own idea anyway.

'I went to see him,' Ross explained, as he started the car. 'And he was quiet, so I told Patience I'd take him with me. He won't be any trouble.'

Karen wasn't too sure about that, but she was so

pleased to see William, and so touched that Ross had done this, that she didn't argue.

'We'll have to watch that he doesn't get in Adam's way,' she said, a little doubtfully. And then, reluctant as she was to spoil this time, she knew she had to tell Ross. Casually, lightly, she said, 'Oh, Adam had quite an outing yesterday. He and Shona went to St Andrews, and—and Adam phoned to say they were staying overnight. They came home this morning.'

She saw Ross's hands tighten on the steering-wheel.

'That was quite adventurous for Adam,' he said after a moment, with careful politeness.

And Karen's heart sank, for the easy warm intimacy between them had gone. But she'd had to tell him. A few moments in their company and he would have known that things had changed between them.

She thought, afterwards, that Ross was glad to have William with them when they arrived at the house. William, by his very presence, created a diversion, and Ross was able to mention, casually, that he believed Adam and Shona had been at St Andrews, while at the same time trying to point out to William that Tess was an old lady who really wasn't too interested in playing games with dogs she hadn't even been introduced to.

But to everyone's relief, William did seem to realise that Adam had to be treated with care. Somehow he seemed to be able to move slowly and carefully when Adam was around, and he didn't jump up at him, or run in front of him.

'You'd almost think he knows,' Shona said wonderingly. 'And knows not to be rough with you either, Mrs Cameron.'

Ross looked at her sharply, and then at his mother. Karen waited for him to make some comment, but he said nothing. But more than once, as they sat at the fire having tea, she saw him glance at his mother, his dark eyes concerned.

As soon as he had had tea he turned to Karen.

'Let's give William a run on the cliffs,' he suggested. 'It'll be dark soon.'

The clouds were grey and threatening, and although it wasn't raining the wind buffeted them as they walked along the cliff path. William ran ahead of them, enjoying the freedom and the interesting smells, but every so often he came back to check on them, before he ran off again.

'Go on, you daft dog!' Ross told him, laughing, and William wagged his tail, taking this as a compliment.

Up here on the wind-torn cliffs, it seemed to Karen that Ross had put everything and everyone else behind him. There were only the two of them, and the dog, in this world bounded by sea and sky and stark cliff. Ross took her hand in his and held it close, when they turned to go back to the house. It was still too wild and windy to speak, and somehow she was glad of that.

When they reached the kitchen door and drew into the porch and out of the wind, they stood still, getting their breath back.

Gently, a little awkwardly, Ross untied the strings of her anorak hood and let it fall back. He touched her flushed cheeks.

'Roses,' he said softly. 'You have wild roses in your cheeks, Karen.'

He looked down at her, and there was something in his eyes that made her heart thud unsteadily. He kissed her then, a warm, deep and slow kiss, and his arms held her very close to him.

Slowly, reluctantly, he released her. But the warmth

and the promise of his kiss was still there in his eyes, when they went inside.

His mother and Shona were in the kitchen, Shona taking a casserole from the oven, his mother cutting bread.

'We thought we'd eat earlier, Ross,' Mrs Cameron said, 'since you have to get back to Edinburgh.'

There was talk, and there was laughter, over the big kitchen table, that evening, and one thing Karen did take in was Adam asking Ross to find out anything he could about the Lincoln surgeon who managed to operate, in spite of a badly injured leg. But most of the time she was in a world of her own, a world where she dared to allow herself to dream that Ross's feelings for her were deeper and stronger than she had thought.

It was a noisy, happy meal. She remembered that later. Adam insisted on helping to dry the dishes, and his mother sat down at the table, drying cutlery. Shona, the dishes finished, went to make sure there were no cups left in the living-room, and Ross said he should phone the hospital.

The radio was on, and suddenly Adam lifted his hand.

'It's that old *Goon Show*, the Christmas Pudding one,' he said. 'Ross loves it—go and tell him it's on, Karen.'

The phone was in the living-room, and the door was half open. Karen, on the point of going in, stopped.

Ross and Shona were standing in front of the fire. Neither of them had seen her.

And as she stood there, Ross put his arms around Shona and drew her to him, her long fair hair against his shoulder, his arms holding her close to him.

Just as he held me, such a short time ago, Karen thought, shaken and heartbroken.

CHAPTER FIFTEEN

NEITHER Ross nor Shona had heard her or seen her.

Karen stood there, and slowly anger began to replace the desperate hurt. Anger not so much for herself as for Adam.

She stepped silently back into the hall then opened and shut one of the other doors. Then she walked, loudly enough to be heard, towards the half-open door.

This time Ross was at one side of the fireplace, and Shona at the other. And neither of them, she thought, looked at all discomposed or ill at ease.

'There's an old *Goon Show* on the radio—Adam thought you might want to hear it,' she told Ross. She lifted two coffee-mugs from the small table and went back to the kitchen.

'Barring emergencies, I have a very short theatre list for Saturday morning,' Ross said, coming in behind her. 'So I should be here mid-morning—we could take William for a good long walk, Karen.'

Karen, rinsing out the last coffee-mugs, said nothing.

'That should be safer than arriving in the middle of the night, and almost being knocked out,' he added, laughter in his voice. 'Mum, I'll have to go now.'

As Karen finished at the sink he turned to Adam— and spoke, Karen thought indignantly, perfectly normally.

'I'll see if I can put you in touch directly with this fellow in Lincoln, Adam,' he said.

'Thanks, Ross,' Adam replied.

In all these weeks since his accident, Karen had never seen him so casual, so relaxed. All at once she could hardly bear to be in the same room as Ross and Shona.

'I'm terribly behind with writing letters,' she said brightly. 'And my mother worries if she doesn't hear from me. If you don't mind, I'll go up to my room and write an airmail. Thanks so much for bringing William here, Ross.'

She saw the surprise on Ross's face as she closed the door. In her room, she sat down on the bed, beyond tears, waiting only to hear him drive off.

An hour later, her letter still unwritten, she went down to ask Adam if he needed any help in getting ready for bed.

'No, thanks,' Adam replied. 'I can manage—and if I can't, I'll give a yell for Shona.'

Mrs Cameron, a slight flush on her cheeks, went on serenely knitting.

'Goodnight, Karen,' she said. 'Ross didn't think of bringing William's basket, but I got him to bring an old one—yes, it belonged to Rufus, Adam—in from the garage, and I've put a blanket in it. William won't mind being in the kitchen, will he?'

'William will sleep anywhere,' Karen told her. She took William through to the kitchen, and showed him the basket. The dog wagged his tail politely and went back to the fire.

'I'll put him through last thing,' said Adam. He looked at her. 'You do look as if you could do with an early night, Karen.'

But an early night just meant a longer night of sleeplessness, Karen found. It was only towards morning that she fell into a heavy, exhausted sleep, to wake unrefreshed.

Adam and Shona were having breakfast when she went down. William greeted her with pleasure, but very much as if he expected her to appear.

'I took Mrs Cameron some tea and toast on a tray,' Shona told her. 'Do you want scrambled egg, Karen? I can do some more.'

Karen shook her head and said tea and toast would do her as well.

'I have to make a couple of phone calls,' Adam said, and reached for his crutches and made his way out of the kitchen, and across the hall.

'I have to stop myself from helping him,' Shona said quietly. She poured more tea for herself and for Karen. 'I suppose you know we spent the night together in St Andrews, Karen?'

Karen nodded, unable to speak.

'Everything's going to be fine,' Shona said, her blue eyes clear. 'We—had to know, you see. We had to be certain.'

Carefully Karen stirred her tea.

'And you are certain?' she asked.

'Oh, yes,' Shona replied. 'Adam knows I love him, he knows it's not pity, or sympathy, or anything else. And he's grown to look at me differently, in this time.'

So why were you in Ross's arms yesterday? Karen thought. But there was no mistaking the shining sincerity on Shona's face. And so—carefully, painfully, she worked it out—it was Ross, then, who had not been able to accept the situation, who had taken Shona in his arms because he couldn't help himself.

And in that moment, Karen knew that second best could never be good enough. If Ross still felt so strongly about Shona, then she would not be able to live with that.

She stood up.

'I think I'll take William for a walk,' she said. 'I'd have time, before taking Adam for physiotherapy.'

'I'll take him today,' Shona offered. 'I want to pick up a couple of things from my flat anyway.'

It was raining, but Karen hardly noticed it. With her hands thrust deep in her pockets, she walked along the cliff path where she and Ross had walked together. William, sobered by the rain, ran only a little way ahead of her.

I can't stay here, Karen thought unhappily. I can't stay, and have Ross coming again the day after tomorrow. I've got to get away.

With her mind made up, she turned and walked back to the house. Mrs Cameron was in the kitchen, an old towel ready to dry William.

'There, you can go and join Tess at the fire now,' she told him. She looked at Karen. 'Is something wrong, dear?' she asked, and the warm concern in her voice was almost too much for Karen.

'Mrs Cameron,' she said with difficulty, 'I did say I'd stay for a fortnight, but I want to go. It shouldn't be difficult, for these last few days. Shona will help Adam, and Ross will be here at the weekend.'

'Oh, Karen, I had thought you'd stay till Sunday night, and then go back with Ross,' said Mrs Cameron, obviously disappointed.

Karen shook her head.

'I—can't,' she said, her voice low.

The dark brown eyes, so like Ross's, studied her. Then Mrs Cameron patted her hand.

'All right, my dear,' she agreed. 'You've given us all this time already. I believe Shona's taking Adam to

Edinburgh—will she be able to fit you and William in too?'

Karen was grateful to her for making no difficulties, and Adam, too, accepted her sudden decision. Shona's clear blue eyes were questioning, and Karen was glad there was no time to talk, as she hurriedly packed her things.

They left early, to allow time to drop Karen at her flat. Just as they were ready to leave, and Karen was about to get into the car beside William, Mrs Cameron took both her hands in hers and kissed her cheek.

'Goodbye, my dear, and thank you for all you've done for us,' she said warmly. 'Not only for Adam, but for me too. I hope you'll come back and see me?'

Karen didn't answer, for she could not be anything but honest with this woman she had grown so fond of. For a moment she saw understanding in the older woman's eyes.

'I wish——' Mrs Cameron began, not quite steadily. 'Goodbye, my dear. At least phone me, will you?'

Karen promised she would.

'Quite an emotional farewell, for my mother,' Adam commented, as they drove down the cliff road, away from the house. 'Pity you feel you can't stay for the weekend—Ross will be disappointed.'

'He'll live with it,' Karen returned, unable to stop herself. Shona, concentrating on the steep road, didn't seem to have heard her, but Adam's grey eyes were questioning, considering.

There was no one at home in the small basement flat, but Karen had expected that Patience would be on duty. She had her own key, and when she had waved goodbye to Adam and Shona she let herself in. William, after a quick check to see if the ginger cat next door was around, seemed quite pleased to be back, and soon settled in his usual place—which was wherever Karen was.

'I'll move back to the hostel tonight,' Patience insisted, when she came off duty and found Karen back. 'There's only one bedroom, after all.'

Karen had made a meal for both of them, and when they had finished Patience phoned her medical student boyfriend, and he came round to take her and her belongings back to the hostel.

'Sorry to come back unexpectedly, and a few days early,' Karen apologised.

'No problem,' Patience assured her. She smiled. 'Let me know if you hear of a flat like this, though—I've enjoyed the freedom.' She patted William's black head. 'And the exercise of taking you out, my boy!'

That night Karen went to bed early, and made up for the sleep she had lost the night before. It had been the right decision to come away, she knew that, and yet she had a strangely disorientated feeling—as if she had left part of herself in the old stone house on the cliffs.

She spent the next morning doing some cleaning and some shopping, and then writing letters she had not been able to do the night she had found Shona in Ross's arms. But by afternoon she was restless, and the empty and lonely weekend stretched out ahead of her.

On an impulse, she phoned the hospital and asked to be put through to Sister Newton.

'I know I'm not due back till Monday,' she said, 'but Patience Mbatha mentioned that you're very short-staffed, and she also said I was back on Women's Surgical—if you needed me, I could come in tomorrow?'

'Staff Nurse Taylor, we certainly do need you,' Sister Newton said thankfully. 'Half my staff are off with this flu, and the other half are either recovering or getting ready to go down with it!'

Karen put down the receiver, glad she had done this. And, apart from filling the empty weekend, it would be easier, she knew, to go back to work while Ross was away. If he had a theatre list, even a short one, on Saturday morning, he was unlikely to have time for a ward round. Mr Wilson would probably do that. So she wouldn't have to see him until Monday. And by then, Karen told herself, I'll feel better in every way.

Sister Newton had not exaggerated her need of extra staff, she found. There was an emergency appendectomy and the patient needed constant naso-gastric suction, and a check for a possible pelvic abscess. There was a femoral hernia which had been repaired, and that patient also needed naso-gastric suction. There were temps to be taken, bedbaths to be done, dressings to be changed, for the more straightforward post-operative patients, and there were two new and very nervous student nurses.

'They take them very young these days, don't they?' Moira commented, from the height of her own twenty-three years. 'Poor kids, thrown head-first into this lot— hey, I'm dying to hear about everything! See you at teatime.'

Karen went on with the catheter she was inserting, and assured her patient that she would feel much more comfortable now.

'It certainly didn't hurt as much as I thought it would,' her patient, a cheerful white-haired woman, said with some surprise. 'My sister had one of these when she had a hysterectomy, and she said it was agony!'

'I'll be back to check it soon, Mrs Phillips,' said Karen, making a note on the chart. 'Oh—I'm sorry, Doctor.'

Turning, she bumped into a tall, white-jacketed figure, and her heart turned over. Ross, striding into the ward, his chin set, his eyes dark and very angry.

'Can I have a word with you, Staff Nurse Taylor?' he said.

'I—certainly, Mr Cameron,' Karen replied, completely thrown by seeing him, when she had thought he would already be on his way to Lochford.

He strode ahead of her out of the ward and into the corridor. Karen had no choice but to follow him.

'What's the meaning of this nonsense?' he asked her. 'If I hadn't phoned my mother just now, I wouldn't have known.'

Karen lifted her chin.

'I wasn't really needed, Mr Cameron,' she said steadily. 'And I wanted to come back. Now, if you'll excuse me, I have work to do.'

His hand closed on her wrist, hard and painful.

'For heaven's sake, Karen, you can't just go like that!' he told her. 'You can't walk out on my brother!'

'Oh, yes, I can, Mr Cameron,' Karen returned. 'He can manage without me—you said yourself he had to be independent.' Swift anger, at the memory of Shona in his arms, strengthened her, and she pulled her arm away. 'I'm sorry, but I really am busy.'

She walked back to the ward, conscious that he was standing there, watching her. And then, abruptly, he turned and walked away, his white coat flying, his strides long and angry.

He'll go down to Lochford, she told herself. And he'll find that I'm right, that they can manage without me.

It was a long, hard day on the ward, but she was glad of that, grateful to be kept occupied, with no time to think. There would just be time enough to take William over to the Gardens before it was too dark, she told herself. Resolutely she pushed away the comparison of the quiet and lonely evening she would have, and the people in the house on the cliff.

She and William were just inside the big wrought-iron gates when William gave a yelp of delight and pulled away from her so unexpectedly that she had no choice but to drop his lead, as he rushed off towards a tall, tracksuited figure.

'I thought I'd find you here,' Ross said, and took the lead from her. 'Wait, William!'

He looked down at her.

'William can have five minutes' exercise,' he told her, 'then we're going to talk, you and I.'

Karen took a deep breath.

'I don't think we have anything to talk about,' she said.

'Perhaps not,' he agreed, 'when you feel you can walk out like that.'

This took her so much by surprise—that he should behave as if he was the one who should feel offended— that she was silent. Ross held William's lead firmly, and William, as before, accepted his authority and walked beautifully. When they reached the open part, Ross let him go, and stood with his hands in the pockets of his tracksuit, watching the big black dog as he ran around.

Karen, not trusting herself to speak, said nothing.

'Home, William,' said Ross, and put the dog's lead on.

I don't have to let him come in, Karen told herself.

'No, Ross,' she said, when they reached the steps to her flat. 'There's no point in this.'

'I think there is,' Ross said, and looked down at her, unsmiling. 'I thought we were friends, Karen.'

He sounded sad, not angry, now, she realised, bewildered. And he had no right to be either.

He took the key from her and opened the door. And then, as he once had before, he untied the hood of her anorak and took it off her. Then he took both her hands in his.

'Why did you go away, Karen?' he asked her, and his voice was gentle now. 'Just when things were—beginning to come right.'

There was no point in pretending, for either of them.

'Because I saw you with Shona in your arms,' she told him wearily.

He was very still. 'And what did you think?' he asked her.

Karen shrugged.

'I thought that in spite of knowing that Shona loves Adam, you—couldn't help yourself, you still loved her, and you were going to lose her.'

He let her hands go.

'Oh, Karen,' he said then. 'Oh, lassie, but you are foolish!'

He put his arm around her shoulders and led her to the couch in front of the fire.

'Sit down,' he said.

For some reason unable to argue, Karen sat down. Ross sat down beside her.

'Will you listen to me?' he asked her. 'I mean really listen?'

Her throat was unaccountably tight, so she nodded.

'Shona told me that everything was wonderful between Adam and her,' he said, his eyes very dark, very intent on her face. 'She said she had no doubts, and that neither had Adam now. She—said she was sorry she'd ever let me think that there could ever be anyone else for her.'

And in spite of everything, Karen was sorry for him.

'Oh, Ross,' she said, not quite steadily, 'I'm sorry.'

'Don't stop listening,' he told her. 'I told her that my mother had suggested to me that it was only because she was Adam's girl that I'd been interested in her at all. The old rivalry thing again. And I told her that, although I told my mother that was nonsense, I'd done a lot of thinking, and I knew she was right.'

He smiled, the slow, warm smile that did such strange things to her.

'Och, she's bonny, there's no doubt about that, and I see now that she's a nice girl, as well as being bonny, but when I allowed myself to accept what my mother was saying I was free. And Karen, that was when I put my arms around her—because I was happy for myself, happy that she was gong to marry my brother.'

Karen closed her eyes, and she could see, once again, that moment when she had stood at the door and looked in on Shona and Ross. And she knew, with complete certainty, that what Ross had just told her was the truth.

'I—don't know what to say,' she said, with difficulty.

But he hadn't finished.

'And there's another thing my mother said,' he told her. 'She said I'd been so stubborn about this, so